Breaking Story

some crimes should go unsolved

John S Ross

Copyright © 2025 John S Ross All rights reserved
The characters and events portrayed in this book are fictitious. Any similarity to real persons, living or dead, is coincidental and not intended by the author.
No part of this book may be reproduced, or stored in a retrieval system, or transmitted in any form or by any means, electronic, mechanical, photocopying, recording, or otherwise, without express written permission of the publisher.
ISBN-13: 9798316142330

Cover design by: fiverr.com - @kingof_designer
Library of Congress Control Number: 2018675309
Printed in the United States of America

chapter one

Saturday. 2.40pm. North Glasgow

Brian opened the shed door wide and stood in the doorway. He was dressed casually in jeans, Celtic football top and denim jacket. Exactly the way he needed to be dressed to blend in where he was going to go shortly.
He was a man with a plan and this was the final preparation for an operation he had planned.
He stood in the doorway for a few seconds silently and quickly scanning the interior of the shed for what he was looking for. He had never been in this shed before as it belonged to a friend of a friend whom he had never met until about half an hour ago.
The hut was fairly small at 15 by 6 feet and was almost full to capacity with all the various stuff you would expect to find in a family garden shed.
The left hand side of the shed was taken up with shelves holding hammers, saws, spanners, nuts, nails, screws etc.
The centre walkway had a mountain bike and a golf bag at the far end.
The right hand side had a waist height work bench that ran the full length of the shed from front to back and was partly covered in the middle by a semi rolled up piece of linoleum.
Brian picked up the linoleum to reveal what he was looking for. An abrasive wheel tool sharpener.
Brian rolled up the piece of linoleum and placed it on one of the shelves on the left hand side of the shed then he

approached the abrasive wheel.

Brian flicked the power switch on the side of the abrasive wheel and the tool sharpener came to life spinning at high speed ready to sharpen something.

Brian reached up his right sleeve with his left hand and took out a 12 inch steel knitting needle ready to be sharpened by the wheel. He paused for a second looking at the needle then he started to sharpen the needle on the wheel.

The needle didn't take long to sharpen and was ready in less than a minute.

When it looked like the needle was sharpened enough Brian switched off the abrasive wheel then tested the sharpness of the needle on his left index finger and it was sharp enough for purpose.

Brain reached into one of the front pockets in his jeans, took out a wine bottle cork and stuck it onto the end of the needle. The needle was now ready.

Brian slipped the needle and the cork up his right sleeve with the cork rubbing against his wrist then closed and locked the shed door and walked away.

Saturday. 3.12pm. North Glasgow

It had now been nearly three quarters of an hour since Brian sharpened the knitting needle with the abrasive wheel and he now found himself in the Craiglen area of North Glasgow standing across the road from the Craiglen Inn pub known locally as the Craigy Inn.

The Craigy Inn was a fairly average looking little pub made of brown bricks. It consisted of a bar and a lounge area, had steel bars over the windows and vitally no CCTV. anywhere.

In the past the pub had a bad reputation for violence and for a while the establishment was known as the flying tumbler because of the regular bar brawls it experienced. But for the last few years it had been pretty quiet with almost no trouble at all because it was now owned by a large and violent crime family from East Glasgow and they had made it known that anyone causing trouble in the pub would be dealt with severely.

It was the worst kept secret in Craiglen that the Craigy Inn was now mob owned.

On this particular Saturday afternoon the Craigy Inn was full to capacity with Celtic fans as Celtic were playing Aberdeen in the Scottish cup final. |The outside of the pub was decorated with green and white scarfs, the colours of Glasgow Celtic F.C. also known as 'Celtic' also known as the 'Celts', also known as 'Cclic', also known as the 'tic', also known as the 'bhoys',and also known as the 'hoops'. A half dozen different names for one football team.

Brian knew the guy he was looking for was an ardent Celtic fan and was going to be in this pub watching the game. He knew this because Brian had been effectively stalking this particular individual on social media and had been absorbing everything he could learn about him.

The guy he was looking for was called Mark Adam or Sparky to his friends and was a member of the street gang the Craiglen Young Team or the CYT for short and he had been planning to meet some friends at the Craigy Inn to watch his beloved Celtic in the big football match.

He had good reason to worry about his personal safety but he would be with a dozen or so friends in the pub and there would be dozens of potential witnesses so he would be feeling safe.

Brian stood across the road from the Craigy Inn for a few seconds finalising in his head what was about to happen. There was no-one outside smoking as the game had just started at 3pm and everyone would be inside watching. And he knew there was no CCTV. in the area as he had already done an extensive check of the area because he knew the first thing the cops would do, after he had done what he had come here to do, would be to check all the CCTV. footage in the area.

Brian reached into the front of his denim jacket and took out a green and white Celtic skip hat, put it on, then started to cross the road towards the pub.

Brian opened the heavy wooden door to the Craigy Inn and entered the premises.

Inside the pub it was mobbed. Probably as many as 100 Celtic fans all dressed in green and white mostly in the bar area, with some others through the back in the pool area, all drinking and shouting at the giant TV. screen on the wall.

Brian quickly scanned through the pub looking for Sparky taking care not to make eye contact with any of the drinkers in the pub. He had memorised a few pictures of Sparky from social media and he knew he was about 6 feet tall, medium build with short ginger hair.

After a few seconds Brian noticed Sparky in the middle of perhaps 50 drinkers standing in the centre of the pub in front of the giant TV. on the wall. He was wearing jeans and a Celtic football top and was drinking from a bottle of beer.

Brian decided to make his move. He slowly walked over towards the centre of the group of drinkers in front of the TV a few steps at a time. After a minute or so he found himself standing directly behind Sparky and he quickly glanced to his left and then to his right making sure everyone nearby was transfixed watching the match on the TV.

After another minute or so Brian held up his right arm to face height and took the cork off the sharpened needle up his sleeve. As lightly as he could he then placed his left hand on Sparky's back on his left shoulder blade with his fingers spread as wide as they would go. Then he very quickly took out the needle, lined it up at a right angle to Sparky's torso and with the tip placed between Brian's index and forefinger then violently slapped the end of the needle forcing it into Sparky.

Brian held the needle in place for a few seconds then turned it a quarter of a turn clockwise, held it again for a few seconds then in a single movement pulled the needle out of Sparky, placed the cork back on the needle and put the needle back up his sleeve.

The needle pierced through Sparky's back, through his heart and out of his chest. It happened so quickly that he hardly felt a thing apart from a stinging sensation on his chest. He held his hand up to the left hand side of his chest where a steadily growing bloodstain had appeared on his shirt.

Brian took a few steps away from Sparky and began to make his way to the door again making sure not to make eye contact with anyone.

Sparky touched the bloodstain on his shirt with his right hand then looked at the blood on his hand. His vision was getting blurry. He leaned a little to the left then staggered away to the right falling onto a table covered in drinks knocking the drinks over the people sitting at the table. There were 2 men and 2 women sitting at the table. Both of the male drinkers sitting at the table stood up and shouted at Sparky clearly unaware that Sparky hadn't had too much to drink, he had in fact been fatally wounded.

"What the fuck?" shouted one.

"What are you doing?" shouted the other.

Brian had seen enough. He pushed open the heavy wooden door and left the pub. Another member of the CYT lay dead on the ground. His work here was done.

chapter two

Monday. 10.15am. Daily Post HQ. Glasgow.

It was 10.15am the Monday morning following the incident at the Craigy Inn and Sarah Gibb was sitting on a seat in the hallway outside the editor's office at the headquarters of the Daily Post newspaper in Glasgow where she had worked as a journalist since she graduated from University just over 6 years ago.
Random people walked past in a rush some carrying folders and paperwork and some were not. She didn't know why she was here, all she knew was that she received an email first thing this morning asking her to report to Bobby McCiver, the Editor's office at 10.15am.
She was dressed smartly as always in a trouser suit and 3 inch heeled shoes with her hair tied up in a bun and a small handbag sitting in her lap.
Between the years she spent at University in the city and her time employed at the Post she had lived in the city long enough to fully understand the local dialect but not long enough for her to lose her own South London accent.
Two smartly dressed men wearing visitor tags exited Bobby McCiver's office and walked past Sarah on their way along the hallway.
Bobby stepped out his office and spoke to Sarah.
"Sarah please come in," he said.
Sarah stood up and walked into Bobby's office.
Bobby's office was spacious and open with views over the Clyde river from all of its windows. Inside the office there

was a large leather swivel chair that Bobby would sit in with his back to the windows, a large wooden desk with a keyboard and computer monitor sitting on it, a pile of paper folders all packed full of documents and two smaller swivel chairs on the near side of the desk.

Bobby was a fairly small and balding man with a pot belly and a moustache. He was wearing a shirt and tie, was in his fifties and had worked at the paper since he left school, slowly working his way up the career ladder until he reached to top.
Bobby sat down in his seat.
"Please take a seat." he said gesturing to Sarah with his hand.
Sarah sat down on one of the smaller swivel chairs on her side of the desk and placed her handbag on the floor.
"So Sarah what do you know about the McCulkin crime family?" he asked.
Sarah coughed gently into her hand to clear her throat before answering.
"The McCulkin crime family was a crime family based in the North and the East of Glasgow in the eighties, nineties and the early two thousands. Headed by Donald McCulkin known as Culk. They were involved in pretty much every type of criminal enterprise you can think of except heroin dealing. Culk saw smack as a dirty drug and wanted nothing to do with it.
He was widely viewed as the last of the old school of gentlemen gangsters because women, children and civilians were never targeted and he paid for the construction of football pitches and tennis courts and funding various local youth organisations in the areas of the city he operated in. He died in 2009 after a long battle with cancer and his crime network disbanded after his death with most

members joining other organised crime groups in the city. He left behind a wife and 3 sons. I wrote an article on his group for the University magazine when I was at Uni." said Sarah.

"I know you did. I've read it and I thought it was a really good piece of journalism. That's why I think you'll be ideal for a special project I'm putting together." said Bobby leaning back into his chair.
"What project is that?" inquired Sarah.
"The 2 men that you saw coming out of my office were Police Scotland CID. looking for some help from the paper with an ongoing situation." offered Bobby.
"OK. What can I do to help?" replied Sarah.
"Have you ever heard of the Craiglen young team also known as the CYT?" asked Bobby.
"No." said Sarah shaking her head slowly.
"They're a street gang operating out of the Craiglen housing estate in the North of Glasgow and four members of their gang have been murdered in the last seven weeks," said Bobby.
Bobby paused for a few seconds before continuing.
"The police are drawing a complete blank in their investigations. No-one seems to know anything and nobody is speaking to the cops." explained Bobby.
"And the police think that the remaining gang members will talk to me?" said Sarah.
"Not you. To your new partner." said Bobby.
"My new partner?" asked Sarah.
"We've been employing the youngest of Donald McCulkin's sons, Calum, on a part time and freelance basis on true crime pieces for about a year now and I'm going to start him full time working with you on this."
"I see." said Sarah.

"The police know we employ him and they have explicitly requested we put him on this case but not to tell him he has been specifically requested. His methods may be a little unorthodox but his insights are razor sharp and he can delve further into the criminal underworld with a single phone call than we can do with six months of grooming an informant. He's a walking encyclopaedia of crime in the West of Scotland and probably further afield." said Bobby.
"I see." said Sarah again.
"You will be working together as a team. You will be the brains and Calum will be the brawn." said Bobby.
As soon as Bobby stopped talking Calum tapped on the office door from outside.
"Come in." said Bobby loud enough to be heard from the corridor outside.
Calum opened the office door and walked in. He was dressed smartly in a suit and white shirt with no tie with the top few buttons on his shirt unfastened and he had a few days stubble on his chin.
At six foot one he was a ruggedly handsome kind of guy. A type more akin to a rugby player than an Armani underwear model and Sarah was instantly attracted to him.
"Calum McCulkin this is Sarah Gibb. You are going to be working together." said Bobby as he introduced the two to each other.
"Nice to meet you." said Calum.
"You too." replied Sarah.
"Am I late?" asked Calum.
"No. Not at all. You're right on time," said Bobby.
"Please take a seat." he continued to Calum gesturing towards the empty seat beside Sarah.
Calum sat down on the empty chair.
"We were just talking about the Craiglen young team. What

do you know about them?" asked Bobby.

Calum took a deep breath before answering.

"They're a street gang of maybe thirty or forty guys in their late teens and early twenties from the Craiglen estate in the North of Glasgow." said Calum.

"So you have heard of them?" asked Bobby.

"Aye. I've heard of them." replied Calum.

"I was just explaining to Sarah that four members of that gang have been murdered in the last seven weeks and the cops don't have the first clue who has been doing it so they've asked for our help." explained Bobby.

"What kind of help?" inquired Calum.

"They've asked for my best researcher, that's you Sarah, and my best true crime correspondent, that's you Calum, to work together to find out what is going on with these murders." said Bobby.

"I'm not sure that I'm the right guy for this job." said Calum.

"And why is that?" asked Bobby.

"These guys are street punks. They spray paint their names on walls and their idea of criminality is shoplifting and stealing car stereos. A different world from the one I know." explained Calum.

"Maybe so," said Bobby.

"But I'm hoping that they'll open up to you out of respect for your family name in a way they wouldn't do to the cops." he continued.

"Maybe." said Calum.

"Nobody seems to know anything about these killings. Are they an escalation of violence between rival street gangs? Have the gang members done something to provoke the wrath of someone further up the criminality food chain?" said Bobby.

"Or possibly some kind of serial killer targeting CYT gang members?" offered Calum.

The way Calum was thinking was that by far the group most commonly targeted by serial killers worldwide, were street prostitutes mostly because in a serial killers' eyes they were dirty, disease spreading, disposable sub-humans. The second most commonly targeted group were usually the homeless because in a serial killers' eyes they were dirty, often drug or alcohol addicted, wastes of space. The thing that the serial killers who target these groups all have in common is the belief that they were doing society a favour in getting rid of these people. A strong argument could be made that because street gangs contribute nothing to society other than crime, violence and general anti-social behaviour, in the areas they operate in, then they would at the very least register on a serial killer's radar.

"The police aren't ruling anything out at this point and neither are we," said Bobby.

"Another worrying aspect of these killings is that they are becoming more brazen. The latest murder was in the Craiglen Inn on Saturday. Including bar staff there were 86 people in the pub at the time of the murder and no-one saw anything." Bobby continued.

"That doesn't mean much. People get murdered all the time in Glasgow and no-one ever sees anything." said Calum.

"This was different. I've just heard directly from the CID that there were 4 undercover drugs squad police officers in the pub at the time of the killing and even they didn't see anything," said Bobby.

Bobby paused for a moment again before continuing. "Nobody seems to know anything and the cops are desperate to make progress in these murders and they are willing to bend the rules to breaking point to make it happen." said Bobby.

Bobby opened up the top drawer in his desk and took out and ID badge on a chain and placed it down on the table in front of Sarah.

"Anyway. This is how it's going to work. Both of you will still work for the newspaper but Sarah you will also be employed by Police Scotland on a temporary basis as a civilian intelligence analyst and you will have access to all police files including records and intelligence files. You will be based in the Maryhill police station and you will be free to come and go as you please," explained Bobby.

Sarah picked up the ID badge from Bobby's desk and looked at it.

"I can't see this investigation lasting more than a week," said Bobby as he leaned over the table and tapped on the small pile of folders sitting on the table near to where Sarah was sitting.

"These are the official police files on the four murders. No-one outside this room is to know that you have them. I suggest you study them before starting your investigation," said Bobby.

Sarah picked up the folders and placed them on her lap.

"That'll be all for now guys." said Bobby.

Sarah and Calum stood up and took a few steps towards the door.

"And guys," said Bobby, pausing for a moment.

"Good luck."

Sarah and Calum exited Bobby's office and started walking along the corridor with Sarah carrying the files.

"Do you need me to carry those?" asked Calum.

"No, I'm fine." replied Sarah.

"We can take those files to my place to study. Better than having someone looking over your shoulder here." offered

Calum.

"OK." replied Sarah.

"Do you have a car?" asked Calum.

"No." answered Sarah.

"That's OK we'll take mine." said Calum.

A couple of minutes later the elevator door to the underground carpark at the Daily Post headquarters opened up and Sarah and Calum stepped out.

All around them were the cars of the newspaper's employees ranging from very small Minis through to the very large Range Rovers and everything in-between.

Calum took his car keys out of his pocket as he walked along the pedestrian walkway through the carpark.

"This is us." said Calum as he raised his key fob up to eye level and pressed the button to disarm the car alarm and unlock the doors.

The hazard lights from the front of Calum's car, a red Porsche 911, flashed and the car alarm beeped to signal that it was now disarmed.

"Nice car." remarked Sarah.

"Thanks." replied Calum.

"911 Carrera?" asked Sarah.

"Sure is." said Calum as he opened the passenger door for Sarah.

Sarah carefully got into the passenger seat in Calum's car and put on the seat belt.

"You know your cars." commented Calum as he got into the driving seat and started the ignition.

"I had three brothers growing up and they were all car nuts. I suppose some of it rubbed off onto me." explained Sarah.

Calum put his car into gear and drove away.

Monday. 1.15pm. West Glasgow.

Calum drove his car off the road and onto the spacious bricked driveway outside his house, a beautiful 4 bed and 2 bathroom detached sandstone 3 storey Victorian villa in an upmarket suburb of Western Glasgow.

In front of the house was a perfectly manicured patch of grass probably fifty by twenty feet with some kind of flowering tree in the centre of a circular section of turf dug out of the grassy area.

The grassy area was surrounded by an equally well manicured eight feet high hedge that ran all the way from the house to the road and along the side of the road from the corner of the garden to the driveway entrance giving some privacy from passing cars on the road outside.

That was about the extent of Calum's front garden. No flowers or decorative plants because Calum had no interest in gardening. He just paid the Polish guy that worked on most of the gardens in the area £40 every two weeks to take care of all the gardening needs. A fair price in Calum's opinion.

Calum got out of the car and quickly made his way around the front of the car to open Sarah's door for her.

"Thanks." said Sarah as she got out of the car with her handbag in one hand and the police files in the other.

Calum closed the car door behind Sarah and walked with her towards the front door to the house.

Sarah noticed the CCTV. cameras on the front and the side of Calum's house.

"This is a really nice house Calum. I'm impressed." she said as they both reached the half dozen stone steps leading up to the front door.

"Well it keeps the rain off my head." remarked Calum as he put the key in the lock and opened the front door.

The burglar alarm in Calum's house started beeping loudly so Calum quickly approached the alarm control panel on the left hand side wall and quickly typed in a six-digit security code to disarm the alarm. The alarm immediately stopped beeping.

"Come in, come in." said Calum to Sarah.

Sarah followed Calum through the house towards the kitchen.

The interior décor of Calum's house could be described as modern and minimalist with lots of neutral colours and lots of cream marble effect fittings. This was a house interior that had been designed and decorated by someone that knew exactly what they were doing. Probably not Calum. Probably an upmarket interior designer and decorator from the city.

Calum walked along the main corridor of his house, closely followed by Sarah, towards the kitchen. All the while Sarah looking left and right at the various decorations. But no flowers or flowerpots. This house was very definitely a man cave that could benefit from a feminine touch.

After a few seconds the pair reached the kitchen area, a large and fully equipped open-plan futuristic white marble effect area centred around a huge aluminium American style fridge freezer with a large island in the middle of the room. Calum switched on the main light as he entered the room.

"You can put the files there." Calum gestured towards the kitchen island.

Sarah placed the files down on the island.

"Can I get you something to drink?" asked Calum.

"Tea? Coffee? Fruit juice? Mineral water?" he continued.

"No I'm fine thanks." replied Sarah.

Calum opened up one of the doors and took out a small bottle of mineral water and removed the lid.

"Can I use your toilet?" asked Sarah.

"Of course you can." replied Calum.

"Through that door. First door on the left." he continued.

Sarah left the room as Calum sipped from the bottle of mineral water and approached the police files sitting on the kitchen island, picking one of them up and opening it.

Calum stood silently in the centre of his kitchen with a bottle of water in one hand and a police case file in another quickly reading through the typed documents and looking over the photograph images included in the file.

Sarah re-entered the room and stopped a few feet away from where Calum was standing.

"Before we get started I think we need to talk about the elephant in the room." she stated.

Calum was puzzled.

"What elephant?" he replied.

"Your car and your house." said Sarah.

"What about them?" asked Calum.

"I know what your car is worth and I have a pretty good idea what your house is worth and there is no way you are paying for them both with your income as a journalist." said Sarah.

"I see," said Calum as he placed the police file back down on the kitchen island.

"It's not what you think. I'm not involved in anything illegal." stated Calum.

"Aren't you?"

"You know who my Dad was don't you?" asked Calum.

"Yes I do." said Sarah.

"And you know he was involved in all kinds of criminality

don't you" said Calum.

"Yes." said Sarah.

"What you probably don't know is that when he found out he had terminal cancer he spent the last 2 years of his life setting up legitimate businesses for his family, my family, so that they would have a comfortable life without needing to get involved in crime." said Calum.

Sarah started nodding her head in agreement.

"My family at the time consisted of my Mum, two brothers, Billy and Scott and me," Calum continued.

"My Mum died 4 years after my dad died. So Mum's legitimate business interests were split between me and my brothers. My oldest brother Billy was murdered 2 years after Mum died so his business interests were split between me and my other brother Scott. Scott died 3 years ago in a motorbike crash and I inherited all of his interests,"

Calum took a deep breath before continuing.

"Some of the legitimate businesses my Dad set up have weathered well over the years and some haven't. Right now I own 3 car dealerships, a carpet and laminate flooring warehouse and a restaurant,"

Calum paused for a moment to give Sarah a chance to take it all in before continuing.

"Financially speaking I don't need this job. I do it because I believe in it. I believe in confronting and exposing evil. Smack dealers and paedo gangs in particular. That's why I do this job." Calum finished.

There was a brief silence before Sarah spoke up.

"I'm sorry to hear about your Mum and your brothers. I didn't know," she said.

"I didn't mean to offend you by asking about your income," she continued.

"I just wanted to know what I'll be working with." she

finished.

"No offence taken." said Calum before taking a swig out of his mineral water bottle.

"So that's my story. What's yours?" asked Calum.

"What do you want to know?" asked Sarah.

"Your accent for a start. South London if I'm not mistaken." said Calum.

"Croydon. Born and bred." stated Sarah.

"And how did you come to be working as a journalist in Glasgow?" asked Calum.

"My family used to holiday up here in Scotland when I was a child and I always loved it so when it was time to choose a university to go to Glasgow was always my first choice. I enjoyed my time at university so much and I made so many good friends that I decided to stay in the city and find a job here rather than go back to London." stated Sarah.

"And how did you get picked to work on this special project? asked Calum.

"I wrote an article years ago about your father for the university magazine. Our boss, Bobby, read it and I suppose he thought we could work well together." said Sarah.

"Cool." stated Calum before taking another swig from his water bottle.

There was a brief silence before Sarah spoke up.

"I suppose we should really make a start," she said as she took a step closer to the kitchen island with the police files on it.

"But where to start?" she exhaled.

"We should start at the beginning," said Calum.

"With the first murder." he continued.

Sarah quickly looked through the folders in front of her, checking the dates attached to each file and picked the one with the earliest opening date.

"That'll be this guy here. Robert Campbell known as Bob. 24 years old," said Sarah as she opened up the file and placed it on the kitchen island worktop so both she and Calum could both see the contents.

"It says here that he wasn't even reported missing by anyone. His body was found in an abandoned warehouse after being brutally tortured before being doused in petrol and set on fire." said Sarah.

Calum picked up a photo from the file and looked at it. The photo was of a corpse burned beyond recognition and chained to a metal chair.

"Someone wanted him to suffer." he said almost too quietly for Sarah to hear.

"That's an understatement. The pathologists report here says that he had been chained to a metal chair, he had holes drilled into at least 3 of his teeth mostly likely with an electric drill, he had 4 fingers on his right hand cut off and then he was doused in petrol and set on fire while still alive." said Sarah.

"A hell of a way to go." said Calum.

"That's by far the most horrific thing I've ever heard of." said Sarah.

"Never underestimate what people are capable of doing to each other." said Calum as he placed the photo back into the file.

Sarah closed the file they were looking at and picked up another.

"Next up is Derek Swanson known as Swanny. 22 years old. He had his throat slit while out walking his dog," said Sarah while handing a photo to Calum.

Calum looked at the photo of a young man lying on a footpath in a large pool of blood.

"There were no defensive injuries and no sign of a struggle. The pathologist suggests he was most likely attacked from behind and almost decapitated by a single injury inflicted by a large bladed instrument." Sarah continued.

"A straightforward execution. No messing around." said Calum as he placed the photograph back into the file.

Sarah closed the file, picked up another, opened it and handed Calum a photograph from inside the file.

Calum studied the photograph. The photograph showed a man lying on the ground with no obvious injuries.

"The third murder victim was David Smith known as Smitty. He was 21 years old and he was strangled in the early hours walking home from a party. Again there was no defensive wounds and the pathologist suggested that he was attacked from behind and strangled with a very thin cord or cable leaving no forensic trace behind." said Sarah.

"Another straightforward killing." said Calum as he put the photograph back into the police file.

Sarah picked up the last of the 4 police files and opened it.

"And last but not least is Mark Adam known as Sparky. He was 25 years old and he spiked through the heart while watching a football match in the Craiglen Inn on Saturday. The spike was estimated to be around 10 millimetres wide and entered his body through his back slightly right of his left shoulder blade, passed directly through his heart and left a puncture wound on his chest. There were 86 people in the pub including bar staff and undercover cops and no-one saw anything" said Sarah.

Calum took the photo from the folder Sarah was holding and studied it. The picture was of Sparky lying on the floor of the Craigy Inn with a large bloodstain on the front of his Celtic shirt.

"A professional hit of the highest calibre. They all were."

said Calum.

"A professional hit?" inquired Sarah.

"Don't professionals use pistols with silencers?" she continued.

"Some do. Some don't. A true professional can kill using just about anything," explained Calum.

"These guys have all got 2 things in common. They were all members of the CYT and they were all killed by someone that knew exactly what they were doing." continued Calum.

Both Calum and Sarah paused for a few seconds.

"So what do we do now?" asked Sarah.

"Now we go and speak to the CYT I need to make a couple of phone calls." said Calum as he took his phone out of his pocket.

Monday. 2.35pm. North Glasgow

Calum and Sarah were in Calum's car driving towards the Craiglen housing estate in the North of Glasgow.
"So what do you know about this guy we're going to meet?" asked Sarah.
"I know his name is Stevie Ralston and he is known as Razzy. I know he is the son of Davie Ralston, a bouncer that used to do debt collection for my dad and I know that Razzy is currently the leader of the CYT" replied Calum.
"And do you think he'll open up to you?" asked Sarah.
"I suppose we're about to find out." replied Calum.
Calum and Sarah were about to delve into the world of gangs and gang members in Glasgow. It was a world that Calum had a pretty good working knowledge of but Sarah knew very little.
The gang culture in Glasgow could be traced back to the late 19th and early 20th century with the razor gangs of the East End and in its heyday in the 1970's almost every street or estate in Glasgow had its own gang with the gangs having names like the Tongs or the Toi. At that time Glasgow had more gangs than London despite London being more than 15 times the size of Glasgow.
It was a world of endless feuds between schemes, a scheme being a street or an estate and the gang members that inhabited them were known as schemies in Glasgow and weedgies or neds or weedgie neds in the rest of Scotland. The situation was that if you were from a certain street or estate you would automatically join the gang based there when you were old enough and you would automatically become sworn enemies of the rival gangs that your territory bordered with.

The feuds were not about drugs or controlling a certain area. They were mostly just about gang rivalry and also tit for tat revenge attacks for violent attacks on members of your own gang.

Even now in the 21st century the weapon of choice for gang members is a knife. Either a lock knife or a butterfly knife or a box cutter knife but occasionally something larger like a machete or a meat cleaver or even a sword.

The reason for this is that knives are very easy to get hold of compared to guns and the penalty for carrying a knife is a fraction of what you can expect for carrying a gun.

Acquiring a gun in Glasgow is a lot like acquiring a kilo of cocaine in the respect that if you really want one and you have the money to pay for it you can get one. You might have to go through 2 or 3 or 4 different people to get it but you can get it. And just like a kilo of cocaine if you get caught in possession of one you can expect to get 5 years in prison. Maybe more.

Gang members were generally in their early teens through to their mid-twenties and the endless wars they waged on each other went a long way towards Glasgow, at one point, being ranked by the World Health Organisation as the murder capital of Europe.

These days the gang scene in Glasgow is a slowly dying one with government funded initiatives like the Scottish Violence Reduction Unit (SVRU) having a real impact on knife crime and gang membership in the city. The scene is dying but is not dead. Not yet.

Gang members can quickly be identified by anyone travelling through a scheme as they usually hang around in groups outside corner shops or at children's swing parks.

The gangs in Glasgow do not have gang colours unlike Los Angeles and other cities with problems with gangs. In

Glasgow gang members are all dressed the same in tracksuits and baseball skip hats with Lacoste and Burberry being the most in demand designer labels but pretty much any make will do.

Calum pulled his car over and parked outside a boarded up shop in Craiglen and applied the handbrake.

"Now what?" asked Sarah.

"Now we wait." replied Calum.

Sarah looked out the passenger window in Calum's car and what she saw was bleak. Abandoned shops with their security shutters down and covered in spray painted graffiti. Lots of council owned houses, many of them with windows or doors boarded up with wood. Concrete everywhere with not a bit of greenery anywhere.

The Glaswegian comedian Billy Connolly joked that there were areas of Glasgow that would look exactly the same after a nuclear war. Craiglen was definitely one of the areas he was talking about.

These kinds of deprived neighbourhoods just produced generation after generation of criminals with most never rising above the mediocre level of criminality but a few would go on to associate with the large crime families these kind of areas also produced.

The street gangs and crime families in these areas had a similar set up. They both thrived in deprived areas, were largely made up with violent young men who had absolutely no fear of going to prison because they had been in and out of prison and young offender institutions their entire lives. Both types of organisation had a very basic hierarchy with generally the most dangerous man calling the shots.

The Scottish crime gangs and families were nowhere near as sophisticated in their set up as the Russians, the Italians or even the Irish. These organisations had various levels of involvement. Soldiers, captains, bosses, underbosses etc. There was none of that in the Scottish crime families and gangs.

The way it usually worked is that a member of a street gang would get jailed and meet up with an associate of one of the crime families also doing time and they would form a working relationship when they got out.

The crime family associate would offer some pretty basic work to the street gang members. Somebody was to get beat up or slashed or maybe someone's car or business premises were to be fire bombed.

If the street gang members could prove themselves then they would get offered better paying work. Usually drugs. Starting off with weed and speed and ecstasy then moving onto coke and ultimately heroin.

Sarah noticed a schemie crossing the road a little in front of where they were parked up. She knew he was a schemie by the way he was dressed, a white shell suit and a Burberry pattern skip cap.

The schemie kept looking around as he approached the car before he reached the driver side of the car.

He tapped on the driver side window.

Calum rolled down the window.

"Are you Calum?" asked the schemie.

"Aye" replied Calum.

"Razzy said he'll meet you along there at number 112," said the schemie as he pointed further along the road.

"First block of flats on the right. Just press the buzzer and they'll let you in." the schemie continued.

"OK" said Calum as he unfastened his seatbelt.

"Do you want to stay here or do you want to come with me?" Calum asked Sarah.

"I'll come with you." said Sarah as she quickly unfastened her seatbelt.

Two minutes later Calum and Sarah were outside the block of flats they were told to go to. The block of flats was 6 storeys high and looked reasonably well looked after.

Calum pressed the buzzer for 112.

A male voice spoke over the intercom system.

"Hello. Who is it?" the voice said.

Calum leaned in closer to the intercom microphone and pressed the speaker button.

"It's Calum McCulkin. I'm here to speak to Razzy." Calum said.

There was a loud buzzing sound and the entrance door to the flats opened and Calum and Sarah walked in and made a start on the 3 flights of concrete stairs to flat 112.

"When we get in here I'll do all the talking." said Calum as he stepped up the first of the stairs.

"OK" replied Sarah.

A minute later Calum and Sarah were standing outside flat 112 waiting to speak to Razzy the current leader of the CYT

The CYT was not a democratic organisation. No-one had voted Razzy to be the leader. He had earned the position by being the hardest guy in the gang at that time mostly because his dad, Davie Ralston, was a pretty good boxer in his day and he had introduced Razzy to boxing from as soon as he was big enough to put on the gloves.

Razzy became a pretty good boxer and had earned himself a reputation at the high school as being a really good fighter and not to be messed with. Then later when he got into the gang scene and started carrying a knife, he was known for slashing people in the blink of an eye.

The flat door was a fairly average white PVC door with a

single tiny spyhole in the middle of the door at eye height. Calum touched Sarah's arm to get her attention and pointed up to the top corner of the wall where a small CCTV camera had been fitted and pointed to exactly where they were standing. Calum also noticed that the doorbell was a Ring.com video doorbell that would be connected to someone inside the flat's phone or tablet. Possibly a few phones or tablets.

The flat they were visiting was in effect the headquarters or at the very least one of the headquarters of the CYT, a safe house, and they didn't take kindly to unwelcome guests like the police or rival gangs.

The intercom system at the main door offered a first line of defence while the CCTV camera and video doorbell offered another.

"Here we go." said Calum as he pressed the doorbell.

Almost immediately Welshy answered the door and the smell of weed being smoked filled the landing that Calum and Sarah were standing on.

Welshy was dressed in a blue tracksuit with a white skip cap. His head was tilted back, his eyes were nearly closed and he was holding a large joint in his right hand. He was very very stoned on weed.

"'C'mon in troops," he said almost struggling to get the words out.

"Follow me." he continued.

Welshy walked slowly along the corridor towards the living room of the flat with Calum and Sarah following him and with the smell of weed being smoked getting stronger and stronger as they walked.

After a few seconds Welshy, Calum and Sarah reached the living room in the centre of the flat where they were greeted by Razzy and another 5 schemies sitting around the living room smoking weed and drinking bottles of Buckfast wine, a favourite tipple of schemies in Glasgow.

The layout of the living room was pretty basic and consisted of a beat up old sofa, a couple of large armchairs and a glass table in the centre of the sitting area.

The armchairs didn't match each other or the sofa and all the furniture was probably picked up from the street when someone was throwing them out.

The glass coffee table was covered in half empty Buckfast bottles, joints in various stages of development and a green glass weed smoking bong.

Razzy was sitting in the middle of the sofa with Tony and Jimbo sitting on either side of him. Each of the 2 chairs were also occupied by Broon and Boab,. Lafferty was sitting on the floor in front of the coffee table and facing the sofa. He was joined by Welshy, the schemie that had just shown Calum and Sarah in.

Razzy and all the schemies were dressed exactly the way you would expect, they were all wearing tracksuits and baseball skip caps. They fitted the typical stereotype of Glasgow schemies perfectly.

Like most stereotypes, the majority of people probably don't fit the profile but a lot do, otherwise the stereotype wouldn't exist. And these schemies that Calum and Sarah were meeting certainly did.

In the living room of the flat the air was thick with weed smoke as Broon and Boab, Welshy and Razzy were all smoking joints.

Razzy was sitting in the middle of the couch and stood up when Calum and Sarah entered the room.

Razzy clicked his fingers and gestured to Broon who was sitting in one of the chairs.

"You. Fucking move," he barked.

"Give our guests a seat." he continued.
Broon slowly got out of the chair and sat down on the floor next to Lafferty and Welshy.
"You too," he said to Boab in the other chair.
Boab complied and got out of the chair and onto the floor.
"Take a seat guys." Razzy said to Calum and Sarah.
Calum and Sarah sat down on the now unoccupied chairs. Razzy picked up one of the Buckfast bottles from the table and took a big swig.
"You must be Calum." said Razzy reaching across the table to shake Calum's hand.
Calum shook Razzy's hand.
"And you must be Razzy." said Calum.
"Guilty as charged." Razzy smiled.
Tony who was sitting on the right of Razzy passed him a joint and Razzy took a large inhalation, held it in for a while then exhaled.
"My Dad says that your Dad was the fucking man back in the day." said Razzy.
"He had his moments." replied Calum.
Razzy reached out to Calum with the joint in his hand offering it to him.
"No thanks." said Calum gesturing a stop sign with his hand.
Razzy reached over to pass the joint to Sarah.
"Not for me either thanks." said Sarah.
There was a brief pause before the conversation continued.
"So what can I do for… what newspaper is it you work for?" asked Razzy.
"The post. The Daily Post." said Calum.
"Right. The Daily Post. What can I do for the Daily Post?" asked Razzy.
"We're investigating the murders of 4 CYT members in the

last 7 weeks. We're interested in hearing an insider's view from the people that knew the victims the best." continued Calum.

"They were all good men." said Razzy.

"Anything else?" asked Calum.

"Like what?" asked Razzy.

"Like who might have wanted to kill them." stated Calum.

Razzy inhaled then exhaled deeply before answering.

"Nobody springs to mind." said Razzy shaking his head as he spoke.

"No new tit for tat feuds with rival gangs? No unpaid drug debts? No moving in on someone else's turf?" asked Calum.

"No. None of that." said Razzy shaking his head again as he spoke.

"What about the first guy that got killed? The fella Campbell" said Calum.

"Bobby Campbell." said Sarah.

"Bob? What about him?" asked Razzy sounding a little surprised.

"He was the first guy targeted and he was the only one that was made to suffer. My gut tells me there's a reason for that. That there's something special about Bob's killing. That this whole situation is somehow connected to him or something that's he's done or been involved in." asked Calum.

Razzy looked over to the Tony on his left for a second, then looked at Broon, Welshy and Lafferty on the floor in front of him, then lastly to Jimbo on his right before answering.

"I have no knowledge of Bob Campbell ever being involved in anything like that." he said plainly.

"Are you sure?" asked Calum.

"I'm sure," replied Razzy.

"Just like I'm sure that we're ready for whoever it is that's hunting us." said Razzy as he reached down the back of his tracksuit bottoms and took out a 10 inch hunting knife then placed it down on the table.

Jimbo on Razzy's right reached into one of his socks and took out a 6 inch lock knife.

"We're all pure ready for anything." he said as he placed the knife down on the table.

"We all are." said Broon on the floor on Razzy's right as he placed a set of brass knuckles with a blade in the thumb position down on the coffee table.

All the schemies present, Boab, Lafferty and Tony on the floor also took out knives and placed them on the table.

"Whoever they are and whenever they come for us we'll be ready for them." said Razzy before taking another large swig from the Buckfast bottle sitting on the coffee table in front of him.

"Well I don't think there's anything else for us to talk about." said Calum as he stood up, took his wallet out of his back pocket, took a business card out of his wallet and handed it to Razzy.

"If you can think of anything else that's relevant to what we've been talking about get in touch. My phone number and email address are both on the card." he continued.

"Will do." said Razzy.

Sarah stood up.

"I'll see you out," said Welshy the schemie that let them into the flat as he stood up and started walking towards the door followed by Calum and Sarah.

"Nice to meet yous." Welshy said as Calum and Sarah walked out the door.

"You too mate." said Calum back.

A minute and a half later Calum and Sarah were back on

the street approaching Calum's car.

"He's fucking lying to me." spat out Calum as he unlocked the car with the key fob.

Calum and Sarah got into Calum's car and Calum started the ignition.

"Are you sure?" asked Sarah.

"Absolutely," said Calum as he started to drive away.

"I was maybe 90 percent sure going in there that the key to the whole thing was the death of the first guy killed, Bob Campbell. Now after Razzy's performance in there I'm 100 percent sure. There's a reason Bob was the first guy targeted and there's a reason he was the only one made to suffer. Either he had done something or was involved in something and that's why he was taken out." said Calum.

"So now what?" inquired Sarah.

"For now we look at this whole thing from a different angle. So far we've looked at it from the victim's point of view maybe we should look at it from the perpetrators point of view." said Calum.

"And how do we do that?" Sarah asked.

"If there have been 4 murders in 7 weeks in the same scheme in Glasgow then I know a guy that will probably know something about them or at least some of them." said Calum.

Calum took his phone out of his jacket pocket and placed it onto the phone cradle fitted to the dashboard of the car.

"I need to make a phone call." said Calum.

Monday. 4pm. Glasgow city centre.

About an hour after Calum and Sarah met with the CYT in the Craiglen estate they were now in an upmarket bar in central Glasgow.
Calum had deliberately picked a bar with an extensive CCTV network, so the guy they were going to meet would feel safe, and also a table in the corner as the guy would want to keep his back to the wall and to keep an eye on anyone approaching them. The guy they were waiting to meet was more than a little bit paranoid because over the years he had crossed pretty much every crime family and street gang in the city and all of them were capable of extracting revenge.
All around the bar drinkers and diners were enjoying a meal or an afternoon drink or both. There were approximately 60 customers in the bar at this time with about 40 of them sitting in pairs or small groups at numbered tables enjoying a meal and the rest either standing at the bar or through the back of the bar at the pool table.
Calum and Sarah had positioned in a corner booth with Calum's back to the wall so he could see anyone entering the bar with Sarah sitting across the table from him.
"So who is this guy that we are going to meet?" asked Sarah.
Calum leaned across the table to speak quietly to Sarah. "His name is Malky. You don't need to now his surname. He was an enforcer for my Dad a while back and when my Dad's gang disbanded Malky decided he was going to be a freelance agent for enforcers all over the city and further afield too. He arranges violence for a living. Beatings, slashings, kneecappings even murders. He's originally from the North of Glasgow so it's highly unlikely that all these

murders could take place in his own backyard and him to know nothing about any of them." Calum said quietly.
Calum leaned back into his seat.
"Don't be surprised when you meet him. He's not going to be what you think. He's just a wee guy. But as the old saying goes it's not the size of the dog in the fight that matters." started Calum.
"It's the size of the fight in the dog." Sarah continued.
Malky entered the pub by the main entrance surrounded by smoke from the smokers smoking outside and the vape fumes from the vapers also vaping outside.
Calum was right. Malky did not look like what she thought a gangland enforcer looked like. He was not a 6 foot 4 and 25 stone silverback gorilla. He was more like 5 foot 8 and maybe 12 stone and with his red Stone Island parka jacket and his Timberland boots he was dressed more like a twenty something football hooligan than a fiftyish businessman.
Maybe he started off as a hooligan many years ago as all violent professionals had to be introduced to violence somehow.
"Here we go." said Calum as he stood up to get Malky's attention.
Malky noticed Calum in the corner of the pub and started walking towards him. Calum started walking towards Malky and they met in the centre of the pub.
Calum reached out to shake Malky's hand and Malky shook his hand.
"It's been a while Calum." Malky said.
"Aye. It's been nearly 6 years." replied Calum.
Calum pointed over to the table Sarah was sitting at.
"I've got us a table in the corner. Just the way I know you like it." said Calum.

Calum and Malky made their way over to the table and introduced Malky and Sarah to each other.

"Sarah this is Malky. Malky this is Sarah." said Calum as he sat down next to Sarah so Malky could have his back to the wall.

"Nice to meet you Malky." said Sarah.

"Nice to meet you too Sarah." said Malky as he slowly sat down at the table.

Malky paused for a second before speaking.

"I didn't know this was going to be a ménage à trois." said Malky.

"Sarah's cool. You can trust her. I wouldn't have brought her along if you couldn't." explained Calum.

Malky paused for a second again before speaking.

"So what can I do for the youngest of the McCulkin brothers?" Malky asked.

"I'm working as a journalist now and I'm investigating 4 murders in the Craiglen area over the last couple of months." said Calum.

"I've heard about them" said Malky nodding his head as he spoke.

"What have you heard?" asked Calum.

"I've heard that 4 members of the CYT have been killed in the last 2 months. I've heard that the first guy killed was tortured then set on fire. Nasty." said Malky.

"What else have you heard?" said Calum.

"Not a lot. I've just heard that another 2 CYT members were killed on the street a week or 2 apart then the latest guy got stabbed to death in the Craigy Inn on Saturday." explained Malky.

"Nothing else?" inquired Calum.

"That's about it." said Malky.

"No theories on who might be behind any of these

killings?" asked Calum.

Malky shook his head as he answered.

"Nope. Nothing," said Malky.

"You're not the first guy to come to me asking about these killings." Malky continued.

"Who else has been asking around about this?" asked Calum.

"The first guy that got killed was from a family I know well. The Campbells from Craiglen. I know his uncles well, we used to be close back in the day and they've been at me looking for info. I told them exactly what I'm telling you and that is that I know nothing about these killings. Absolutely nothing. Whoever is setting these killings up and whoever is committing them is someone I don't know," said Malky.

There was a brief pause before Malky continued.

"Have you considered it might just be an escalation of a feud between rival gangs?" asked Malky.

"Both of us know members of these schemie gangs always carry knives. Maybe it's just them killing each other." Malky continued.

"No. I don't think so. These murders were committed by someone that knew exactly what they were doing. Especially the last murder in the Craigy Inn." said Calum.

"The guy that got stabbed watching the football?" asked Malky.

"Aye. He was killed by a single injury that no-one saw being inflicted." said Calum.

"That's always the way though isn't it? People get stabbed to death all the time in Glasgow and no-one ever sees anything." said Malky.

"This time it was different. There were 4 undercover drug squad officers in the pub at the time of the murder.

Professional observers watching everything and everyone and even they didn't see anything." said Calum.

"I didn't know about the cops being there. That changes things. Maybe it was someone that knew what they were doing that killed that guy." said Malky.

"Is there nothing you can tell us or no-one you can send us to speak to about this?" asked Calum.

Malky paused before answering.

"There's a guy, Ricky Sloane, that used to work for me that I washed my hands of when I found out he was on the gear." started Malky.

"Heroin?" said Sarah.

"Aye. Heroin. He used to be good at what he did until he picked up a heroin habit, the last time he got locked up. Then he started getting sloppy so I ended our working relationship," said Malky.

"I was going to take him out myself as a precaution in case he started to blab about the work he used to do for me but his best mate pleaded with me not to. He said that if Ricky ever looked like he was going to talk then he would take him out for me." Malky continued.

"And you think he might be involved in these killings?" asked Calum.

"I think it's a possibility. He's experienced and he always uses a knife these days ever since he was blacklisted by all the gun guys in the city because of his habit. And importantly, he'll work for smack money. A few hundred quid here and a few hundred quid there. He's at the bottom of the food chain these days." replied Malky.

"And how do I get in touch with this guy?" asked Calum.

"You'll need to go through the guy he works for now. His handler. A nasty piece of work from the drum called Davie Dundas." replied Malky.

"The drum? You mean Drumchapel?" asked Sarah.
"That's right. Drumchapel." replied Malky.
"Tell me about this guy Ricky works for now." asked Calum.
"Davie Dundas will be in his early fifties now and his main income is from dealing £20 bags of smack and arranging the occasional beating or slashing, always committed by one of his junkie customers." said Malky
"Like this guy Ricky Sloane you were talking about." inquired Calum.
"Exactly like Ricky Sloane." replied Malky nodding his head as he spoke.
"Davie Dundas is pretty near the bottom of the food chain himself. He doesn't have any quality guys working for him." Malky continued.
"So how do I make contact with this Davie Dundas character?" asked Calum.
"He operates out of the pool room in the Clachan bar in Drumchapel from opening time to closing time all day every day." said Malky.
"And how will I know him?" asked Calum.
"He's in his early fifties, about 6 foot 2, fairly skinny built, blondie brown shoulder length hair slicked back into a mullet, he's usually clean shaven, he always wears a full length leather trench coat and he's always accompanied by 2 henchmen wherever he goes." detailed Malky.
"That's good info. Anything else I need to know?" asked Calum.
"Try not to piss him off. Don't try to bully or harass him. The henchmen that shadow him wherever he goes are not hired for their sparkling personalities. They're there because they're extremely violent and they are always armed with something like a machete or an axe. They are

usually junkies or psychopaths that don't give a fuck about the consequences of things and they wouldn't give a fuck what your family name is." explained Malky.
"Got it." said Calum.
Malky paused for a few seconds before continuing.
"Is there anything else I can help you with?" asked Malky.
"No. That's about it mate." replied Calum.
Malky stood up and reached across the table to shake Calum's hand. Calum also stood up and shook Malky's hand.
"Good to see you again Calum." said Malky.
"And you too mate." replied Calum.
"It was nice to meet you Sarah." said Malky.
"And it was nice to meet you Malky." replied Sarah.
Malky stepped to his right away from the table and walked towards the entrance/exit of the bar.
"Now what?" asked Sarah.
Calum looked at his watch before answering.
"Now we call it a day. I'll drop you off and I'll pick you up tomorrow afternoon at about 1 o'clock and we'll pay this Davie Dundas character a visit." replied Calum as he stepped away from the table.
"Sounds like a plan." continued Sarah as she also stepped away from the table.

Monday. 5.20pm. South Glasgow

Calum was driving his car through the Shawlands area in the South of Glasgow towards Sarah's home. Sarah sat beside him in the passenger seat.
"Take the next left." said Sarah pointing to a turning in the road coming up.
Calum turned his car down to the left towards some upmarket looking "yuppie" flats.
"This is me just down here." said Sarah pointing to a block of flats coming up on the right.
Calum pulled his car over and stopped.
"That looks like quite a cool wee bachelorette pad you've got there." said Calum.
"Thanks," replied Sarah.
"It's not just mine. I've got a flatmate that stays with me. A friend from uni." she continued.
"Cool." said Calum.
"Do you want to pop in for a coffee?" asked Sarah.
"No thanks." said Calum.
"Some other time though." he continued.
"Sure." said Sarah.
"So I'll pick you up here at 1 o'clock tomorrow afternoon and we'll go and meet up with this Dundas guy." said Calum.
"Ok" said Sarah as she started to open the door to get out.
"There is just one thing I need from you." said Calum.
"Name it." said Sarah.
"I need you to print me off a photograph of a child that has been badly hurt with lots of bruising and possibly an arm or a leg in a plaster cast. It can be a boy or a girl and preferably aged 10 to 12 years old." said Calum.
Sarah was baffled.
"Why?" she asked.

"For motivation." replied Calum.

Sarah was still baffled.

"Motivation?" she asked.

"Trust me. Everything will make sense tomorrow." said Calum.

"Ok then." said Sarah as she stepped out the car and closed the car door.

Calum drove off into the distance.

Sarah crossed the road towards her flat and made her way up a flight of steps towards her flat.

Sarah opened the door to her flat and stepped inside. She picked up some mail sitting on a small table on the left hand side of the door and walked along the short corridor that led towards the living room.

The corridor décor was pretty plain with laminated flooring and whitewashed walls with a picture hanging on the left hand side about halfway along.

Sarah opened the door to the living room and sat down on one of the two leather couches in the room while looking through the mail. It was mostly junk mail. Nothing of any real interest.

The living room was nicely decorated with white walls, a tasteful painting hanging on one of the walls and a large mirror hanging on the another of the walls, 2 leather couches, large TV in the corner and a large glass coffee table with a vase full of flowers in the centre of the room.

Sarah leaned back into the sofa, closed her eyes and took a deep breath in through her nose and out through her mouth. When she opened her eyes her flatmate Lorna was standing in front of her wearing just a large towel around her chest and another around her head.

"I never heard you come in," said Lorna.

"I was just having a quick shower before dinner." she

continued.

Sarah and Lorna had been friends since their first year at University where Sarah was studying journalism and Lorna was studying accountancy.

When it came time to buy a home it was always going to be a place and a mortgage that they could share.

They were more like sisters than best friends and they told each other everything that was going on in their lives. The good the bad and the ugly.

"I'm just in a minute ago." replied Sarah.

Lorna took the towel off her head and started to dry her hair whilst looking into the mirror.

"So how was your day?" Lorna asked.

Sarah paused for a second before answering.

"Interesting. Eventful." Sarah replied.

"Really?" asked Lorna.

"Do tell." she continued while still drying her hair.

"Have you ever heard of Donald McCulkin?" asked Sarah.

"Of course," said Lorna.

"The former Glasgow criminal godfather. Died about 15 years back." she continued.

"I've been paired up with his youngest son Calum at work investigating a group of murders in the North of the city. It's all very hush hush." said Sarah.

Lorna stopped drying her hair and quickly wrapped her hair back up into the towel.

"Stop right there," she said to Sarah.

"I'll get the wine." she continued as she made her way through to the kitchen where she came back a few seconds later with a bottle of wine and 2 glasses and sat them down on the table.

"It's a little bit early for wine don't you think?" asked Sarah.

"It's always wine o'clock with me, you should know that by now," replied Lorna.

"Now tell me all about it." said Lorna as she poured some wine into the 2 glasses on the coffee table.

Sarah took a small sip from one of the glasses in front of her before starting to talk. She knew Lorna would be fascinated by what she was doing with Calum as she loved true crime documentaries and crime dramas and this situation could be classed as both.

"Start from the beginning." said Lorna.

"It all started first thing this morning when I received an email telling me to report to my editor's office at 10.15, which I did," started Sarah.

Lorna took a sip from her wine glass.

"When I get there he invites me into his office and asks me what I know about the McCulkin crime family and I told him what I knew. Then he tells me the newspaper is working closely with Police Scotland on a group of unsolved murders in the North of Glasgow and he wants me to work closely with Calum McCulkin, the youngest son of Donald McCulkin. Apparently Calum has been doing some freelance work for the paper for some time and now he was being taken on full time to investigate these murders," said Sarah before talking a sip of wine.

"Then Calum tapped on my editor's door and my editor let him in." Sarah continued.

"What was your first impression of Calum? Does he have a bad boy vibe going on?" inquired Lorna.

Sarah paused for a few seconds before answering.

"I wouldn't say he has a bad boy vibe but I must admit I thought he was very handsome," replied Sarah.

"Very masculine. Not a boy. Definitely a man." she continued.

"Then what happened?" asked Lorna.
"Then he asked Calum if he had heard of the CYT." said Sarah.
"The CYT?" asked Lorna.
"The Craiglen Young Team. A street gang operating out of the Craiglen area in the North of Glasgow."
"Never heard of them." said Lorna.
"Me neither," said Sarah.
"But Calum had and apparently four of its members have been murdered in the last seven weeks and the cops don't have the first clue who's been doing it. So in desperation the cops have approached the newspaper for help asking that they put Calum on the story because he has a lot of contacts in the underworld and his family name is still very highly respected and crooks and gang members would be more likely to open up to him," said Sarah.
Sarah took another sip from her wine glass before continuing.
"My editor, Bobby, says the cops are willing to bend the rules to breaking point to stop the killings and he wants me to be the brains to Calum's brawn. The cops have issued me with a Civilian Intelligence Analyst pass that will give me access to all the police files I need to see." said Sarah.
"Fascinating," said Lorna engrossed in the story.
"And then what happened?" asked Lorna.
"And then we got in his car and he drove us to his house to look at some paperwork and to plan our next move." answered Sarah.
"What kind of car does he drive?" asked Lorna.
"A red Porsche 911 Carrera." answered Sarah.
"He drives a Porsche?" said Lorna excitedly.
"Yes. He does." said Sarah.
"And what is his house like?" asked Lorna.

"He's got a big place in the West End. Detached. Victorian. At least three quarter of a million quids worth. Maybe more." said Sarah.

"And what's it like inside?" asked Lorna.

"It's really nice. Modern. Minimalist. Could probably use a women's touch." replied Sarah.

"How the hell can he afford that car and that house on a journalist's salary?" asked Lorna.

"I asked him that exact question." said Sarah.

"And what did he say?" asked Lorna.

"He explained to me that for the last couple of years of his life, when he knew he was dying, his dad set up legitimate businesses for his family. For Calum, his 2 brothers and his mum so they could live a comfortable life without getting involved in crime. And as the last living member of his family, Calum inherited all of the businesses that still exist. That's 3 car dealerships, a carpet and laminate flooring warehouse and a restaurant. He told me he doesn't need the journalist's salary. He said that he does the job because he believes in it especially when he can expose paedo gangs and smack dealers." said Sarah.

Sarah took another sip of her wine.

"So what happened next at his house?" inquired Lorna.

"After we looked through the paperwork we decided we needed to talk to the CYT directly so Calum made a couple of phone calls and we were on our way to Craiglen to talk to leader of the CYT A guy called Razzy." said Sarah.

"And then what?" Lorna asked.

"We arrived in Craiglen and were told to go to a flat and ask for Razzy on the intercom which we did. The flat we were directed to was just a shell of a building with a beat up old couch and a couple of beat up old chairs in the living room. There were probably about 8 gang members in the

flat including Razzy all dressed the same and all drinking Buckfast and smoking weed." said Sarah.
"What was Razzy like?" asked Lorna.
"He was in his mid-twenties, average height and build and a bit pasty faced. He looked like he could do with seeing some sunlight." replied Sarah.
"And then what?" asked Lorna again.
"Razzy claimed he had no idea who was killing his friends or why, but Calum doesn't believe him." said Sarah.
"Doesn't he?" asked Lorna.
"No he doesn't," replied Sarah.
"So next we went to speak to a guy called Malky that Calum knows who used to be a gangland enforcer but now arranges violence freelance for gangs and families all over the city and further afield. Calum thought Malky might know something because all of the killings happened basically in his back yard in the North of Glasgow. But he didn't know anything. All he could do is offer us the name of a guy that might be involved, a hitman that is now a junkie and will work for smack money." continued Sarah.
"This is all fascinating stuff." said Lorna totally engrossed in what she was hearing.
"And it will be another interesting day tomorrow as we're visiting a drug dealer so we can get contact information on the junkie hitman and then we'll be visiting the hitman to try and work out if he is involved in the killings." said Sarah.
"Cool" said Lorna as she took another drink from her wineglass.
"Is he married?" asked Lorna.
"I don't think so," replied Sarah.
"He doesn't wear a wedding ring." she continued.
"Girlfriend?" asked Lorna.

"I have no idea," replied Sarah again.

"If he does have a girlfriend I don't think she stays with him. His home is very much a man cave. Definitely missing a woman's touch." Sarah continued.

There was a short pause before Lorna spoke up.

"So I suppose the burning question that needs to be asked is are you going to shag him?" asked Lorna.

"No!" snapped Sarah.

"No no no," she continued as she lay back into the sofa and took another drink from her wineglass and smiled mischievously.

"Well maybe." Sarah almost laughing out loud as she said it.

"I knew it!" said Lorna.

"I knew it." Lorna said again laughing.

After a few seconds the laughing calmed down.

"Calum did say one thing or I should say asked one thing that puzzled me though." said Sarah.

"And what was that?" asked Lorna.

"He asked me to print off a photograph of a child preferably aged 10 to 12 that had been badly bruised and with at least one arm or one leg in a plaster cast." said Sarah.

"Why?" asked Lorna.

"He said it's for motivation but I don't see how it would motivate me or him." said Sarah.

"Weird" said Lorna.

"I have to trust that he knows what he's doing. This is his world not mine." said Sarah.

Monday. 8pm. West Glasgow

Calum stepped into the bedroom in his house that he had converted into a gym for his almost daily workout. His home gym consisted of a running machine treadmill, a static exercise bike, a weights bench, a rowing machine and an abdominal board. He worked out every day Monday to Saturday and he rested on a Sunday.

He was dressed in dark tracksuit bottoms and a loose fitting white T-shirt ready to do some sweating.

It was a Monday and that meant he would start off with a 10km run on the running machine treadmill. Mondays, Wednesdays and Fridays he would start off with a 10km run on the running machine while on Tuesdays, Thursdays and Saturdays he would start off with a 12km cycle on the exercise bike.

Calum stepped onto the treadmill and switched it on. The treadmill started up fairly slowly at first with Calum walking fast to keep up. After a minute or so Calum turned the speed up on the treadmill so he had to jog to keep up. After another minute or so Calum turned the speed up again so he then had to run to keep up.

As the blood started pumping fast through Calum's veins his mind started to race.

Why was Bob Campbell the only victim made to suffer?

Why were other victims basically executed with no fuss?

Why was Razzy and the CYT lying to him?

What was the connection between all the victims?

If they were all killed by professionals who is paying for the killings and why?

These questions swirled around and around in Calum's head with no obvious answer to any of them.

Before he knew it the alarm on the running machine went off telling him that he had completed the 10km run so he moved onto the rowing machine and started on that.
Rowing and rowing again starting off reasonably slow then speeding up as the adrenaline coursed through his veins.
Again the questions plagued him.
Why was Bob Campbell the only victim made to suffer?
Why were other victims basically executed with no fuss?
Why was Razzy and the CYT lying to him?
What was the connection between all the victims?
If they were all killed by professionals who is paying for the killings and why?
After 15 minutes or so on the rowing machine he moved onto the abdominal board.
By now he was sweating profusely with the throat area down to the centre area of his chest and the armpits area of his T-shirt were soaked in sweat but Calum wasn't finished yet. He still had 3 groups of 50 sit ups to do.
He sat down on the abdominal workout board and lowered himself back with all of his fingers touching the sides of his head and pulled himself up using just his abdominal muscles exhaling loudly as he did so.
Again and again he lowered himself down and pulled himself back up exhaling loudly every time. And every time he exercised he kept thinking about the questions surrounding the killings.
Why was Bob Campbell the only victim made to suffer?
Why were other victims basically executed with no fuss?
Why was Razzy and the CYT lying to him?
What was the connection between all the victims?
If they were all killed by professionals who is paying for the killings and why?

After a few minutes Calum finished his sit ups and moved onto the weights bench.

On this particular occasion Calum decided to just do a few butterfly repetitions to work on his pecs and not to do any leg curls or bench presses. He decided that 3 groups of 50 reps would be enough this time. He lay flat on the weights bench and placed his arms behind the pads on the hinged butterfly weights bars on either side of him.

Calum quickly made his way through the first set of 50 reps and stopped for a minute or so to rest and to catch his breath before starting again. The second of the 3 groups of butterfly repetitions took slightly longer than the first as Calum was getting tired. Again Calum stopped for a minute or so to rest and to catch his breath before starting the final set of butterfly reps all the time thinking about the killings. Eventually Calum finished the third set of butterfly reps and sat up on the weights bench panting for breath. His workout was over. Time for a shower.

5 minutes later Calum was in a steaming hot shower. His eyes were closed and the water was spraying onto his face. He was deep in thought thinking about the killings.

Why was Bob Campbell the only victim made to suffer?

Why were other victims basically executed with no fuss?

Why was Razzy and the CYT lying to him?

What was the connection between all the victims?

If they were all killed by professionals who is paying for the killings and why?

10 minutes later Calum was out the shower and drying himself off in the bathroom with one towel wrapped around his waist and another getting used to dry his upper body. He wiped the condensation away from the large mirror above the sink and stared at himself.

He was getting obsessed with these killings and he knew it.

chapter three

1pm. Tuesday. South Glasgow

It was a typical rainy Tuesday afternoon in the Shawlands area of South Glasgow and Sarah was sheltering in a bus stop waiting for Calum to come and pick her up. She was dressed smartly in a trouser suit and trench coat as she always was for work.
All around the area traffic flowed to the left and to the right. Cars, buses and lorries all making their way to their destinations regardless of the weather and all splashing water onto any pedestrians unlucky enough to be walking on the pavement close to a pothole puddle on the road.
After a couple of minutes Calum pulled his car over to the bus stop allowing Sarah room to open the door and to get in.
Sarah opened the car passenger side door and got in.
"Nice weather." said Calum.
"Lovely." replied Sarah.
Calum was dressed casually in a pair of jeans, a white polo shirt and a black leather jacket.
Calum put the car in gear and began to drive away.
"Did you get me that photo I asked you to get?" asked Calum.
"Sure did." said Sarah as she reached into her jacket inside pocket and took out an A4 sized photograph and showed Calum.
Calum quickly looked at the photo of a young girl with her upper body severely bruised, her jaw wired up and her right

in arm in a plaster cast.
"I got it from a plastic surgery website. Apparently this little girl got trampled by a horse freaking out inside a stable." Sarah continued.
"That'll do." quipped Calum.

"I really want to know why you need this photo Calum. I can't see how it will motivate me or you to do anything." said Sarah assertively.
"It's not to motivate you or me. It's to motivate this Davie Dundas character we're going to meet." Calum explained.
"I still don't get it." said Sarah.
"If we can't bully or harass him into talking maybe we can manipulate him." Calum further explained then waited for a reply from Sarah.
No reply from Sarah.
"The first rule in trying to locate a criminal in Glasgow is this. If you tell people the guy you are looking for robbed a bank or killed somebody nobody will want anything to do with it but if you tell people that the guy you are looking for hurt a child then people will be a lot more willing to open up to you." said Calum tapping on the photo still in Sarah's hand.
"Got it now." remarked Sarah as she now fully understood the situation.
Calum continued driving his car towards Drumchapel aka the Drum.
"I've been thinking quite a lot about this whole situation in general and the guy we're trying to locate in particular. Actually I've thought about nothing else all night." remarked Calum.
"And?" asked Sarah.
"I don't think this is the guy who did these killings at all. I think we're barking up the wrong tree." said Calum.

"Why?" asked Sarah.

"I just don't think it's him. All of the killings especially the one in the Craigy Inn were committed by a pro or pros, not some desperate junkie. The guy or guys that committed these killings knew exactly what they were doing and were professional enough not to get seen or to leave behind any witnesses or forensic material." said Calum.

"So why are we going to interview him?" asked Sarah.

"Because he might know something. Maybe he was offered one or more of the jobs or maybe he might know what the link between all the dead gang members is." said Calum.

"Possibly." remarked Sarah.

1.35pm. Tuesday. North West Glasgow

Calum had been driving his car for around half an hour towards the Clachan bar in Drumchapel when he spotted it further along the road.
"That's the place." he said pointing at the pub further along the road on the right hand side.
The bar itself was a fairly run down little pub with bars on the windows, a large name sign above the entrance that had seen better days and a car park on the side of the pub.
Calum drove his car into the car park attached to the pub and parked up.
The car park was probably big enough for 10 cars but there were only 3 cars in the car park including Calum's. The other 2 cars were a silver Vauxhall Insignia and a black Ford Mondeo.
Calum and Sarah got out of Calum's car and started walking towards the entrance. It was still raining so they moved quickly to get inside the pub and out of the rain.
"When we get in here I'll do all the talking," Calum said.
"I know what makes these people tick. I know how they think." he continued.
"Ok." replied Sarah.
"Give me the photo." said Calum with his open hand reaching towards Sarah.
Sarah passed the photo to Calum who slipped it into his inside jacket pocket.
Calum and Sarah reached the entrance to the Clachan pub and walked past a couple of smokers standing in the doorway sheltering from the rain.
One of the smokers was an elderly man in his sixties dressed smartly in a shirt and tie under a jersey and smoking a roll up cigarette and the other smoker looked like a junkie in his twenties dressed in jeans and a denim

jacket and smoking a joint.

Calum thought the junkie, if he was a junkie, might be a lookout for Davie Dundas inside the pub keeping an eye out for the cops for him.

Calum and Sarah entered the pub.

Inside the pub there were maybe half a dozen elderly drinkers dressed similarly as the guy at the front door and they were all sitting at small round tables with most of them drinking pints of beer. One of the drinkers was reading from a newspaper outstretched over the table in front of him while another sat at the bar talking to the barman.

The barman himself was a fairly rough looking character in his early fifties with black curly hair and a big scar down the left hand side of his face.

"Can I help you?" asked the barman.

"We're looking for the pool room." replied Calum.

The barman silently pointed to a door at the end of the bar. Calum and Sarah walked towards the door to the pool room.

"Thanks." said Calum to the barman.

Calum and then Sarah walked through the doorway to the pub pool room.

Inside the pool room Davie Dundas was playing pool with Kermit, a young man in his twenties from the local area and both were being watched by Davie's two henchmen.

Davie Dundas was exactly as Malky had described him. He was in his early fifties, about 6 foot 2, fairly skinny built, blondie brown shoulder length hair slicked back into a mullet, he was clean shaven and he was wearing a full length leather trench coat.

Kermit was about 5 foot 8 and was fairly smartly dressed in Armani jeans, Burberry jersey and Timberland boots. A bit too nicely dressed for a junkie so he probably wasn't a junkie. Maybe he was just an acquaintance of Davie Dundas.

One of Davie Dundas's henchmen sat on a stool in the far corner of the room sipping a pint of beer and watching the pool match. He was in his thirties and was dressed in denim jeans and jacket. He had a dead look in his eyes like there was nothing going on at all in his head. He had the thousand yard stare look normally reserved for ex-military personnel that had seen a lot of action.

Calum remembered that Malky had said that Davie Dundas only hires junkies or psychopaths to watch his back. This guy was probably a psychopath as he didn't look like a junkie.

The second of Davie Dundas's henchmen stood in the other corner behind the pool table and was different from the first. He was dressed in jeans, a black bubble jacket and beat up old nike trainers.

This guy might be a junkie as he had the tell-tale sucked in cheeks that many junkies have and he was constantly scratching himself. His throat, his head, his arms etc.

Davie was about to take a shot at pool when Calum spoke up.

"Davie Dundas?" asked Calum.

"Who wants to know?" replied Davie as he took his shot on the pool table.

"Calum McCulkin." said Calum.

"You probably knew my Dad, Donald." Calum continued.

"Culk?" asked Davie.

"Aye. Culk." said Calum.

Davie stood up straight and smiled.

"Well well well," said Davie.

"If I knew I was going to be meeting criminal royalty today I'd have worn a tie." he continued.

Kermit leaned across the table to take his turn at pool.

"So tell me what I can do for the son of Culk?" asked Davie.

"We're interested in speaking to a guy you know. A guy that works for you now and again." explained Calum.

"Exactly who is looking for this guy I might know and why are you looking for him?" asked Davie.

"It's me and my colleague here Sarah that are looking for him. We're journalists and we believe he might be involved in an ongoing crime story we're working on." explained Calum.

"I see." replied Davie before playing another shot at the pool table.

After Davie played his shot he stood up straight again to speak to Calum.

"And what is this guy's name?" asked Davie.

"Richard Sloane known as Ricky." stated Calum.

"Ricky Sloane?" asked Davie.

"That's right." replied Calum.

Davie paused for a few seconds before answering.

"I don't remember ever meeting anyone called Ricky Sloane." Davie eventually replied before leaning over the pool table to take his turn.

Calum took a step closer to the pool table and reached into his inside jacket pocket.

"I've got something here that might refresh your memory." he said as he reached into the jacket pocket with his right hand.

Both of Davie's henchmen suddenly sprung to life each taking a couple of steps towards the pool table with both of them reaching into their own inside jacket pockets ready to produce a weapon of some type.

"Relax guys it's just a photograph." said Calum as he slowly pulled out the photograph that Sarah had just given him.

Davie's henchmen both stepped back into their earlier positions as soon as they saw it was just a photo in Calum's hand.

Calum reached across the table and handed the photo to Davie.

Davie took the photo from Calum.

"What am I looking at?" asked Davie.

"You are looking at Ricky Sloane's handiwork. Allegedly." said Calum.

Davie stared at the photo.

Kermit walked over for a quick look and walked away slowly shaking his head slowly in disapproval.

"Ricky did this?" asked Davie.

"Allegedly." said Calum.

Davie paused for a few seconds before speaking.

"You're right he does work for me on and off but I've been unable to get hold of him for the last 2 weeks," said Davie.

"His phone number just jumps straight to voicemail and doesn't even ring. He's probably sold his phone for smack money." Davie continued.

"Is there some other way we can reach him?" asked Calum.

Davie stared intensely at Calum before replying.

"Have you got a pen?" Davie asked.

"Sure." said Calum before slowly reaching into his inside jacket again and pulling out a Bic pen and handing it to Davie.

Davie placed the photograph onto the pool table ready to write some information out onto the blank side.

Davie began to write.

"You tell him from me that he's a worthless unreliable junkie fuck up and that he should just lose my phone number if he hasn't already because I want nothing more to do with him." Davie spat out as he handed the photograph and the pen back to Calum.
Calum looked down at the information written on the back of the photograph.
"Is this his current address?" asked Calum.
"It was 3 weeks ago the last time I saw him." replied Davie.
"Thanks for your help Davie." said Calum as he started to walk away.
"Anytime." replied Davie.
Calum and Sarah walked out of the pub and round the corner towards Calum's parked car.
Calum looked down at the information written on the photograph.
"I know this block of flats, it's about 10 minutes away." said Calum.
Calum opened his car with the remote key and both Calum and Sarah got into his car. Calum reversed his car in a semi-circle then drove forwards out of the pub car park.

2.10 pm. Tuesday. North West Glasgow

Calum parked his car in the car park outside a large block of flats and got out the car followed by Sarah.

Both of them looked up at the large building of more than 10 storeys.

"What number does this guy live in?" asked Sarah.

Calum quickly glanced at the photo with the writing on it.

"Fourteen," said Calum.

"There's 2 addresses to each floor so our guy will be on the 7th floor." he continued.

Calum and Sarah walked over to the entrance to the flats, a solid steel door with an intercom system on the right hand side.

Calum pressed the button for flat 14 and the intercom system started making long beeping sounds alerting the occupant of flat 14 that there was somebody wanting to speak to him at the main door to the building.

After 30 seconds or so the intercom stopped beeping. Calum pressed the button again and again the intercom system started making long beeping sounds and again no-one answered the intercom alert.

"Now what?" asked Sarah.

"Now we wait," said Calum.

"Sooner or later someone is going to open this door and we'll just slip in." he continued.

"You seem fairly eager to speak to this guy considering you are sure this isn't the guy that we're looking for." said Sarah.

"I don't think he did any of these murders but I think he might know who did at least one of them or who was looking to get these guys done in. It's worth a try." replied Calum.

Calum and Sarah didn't have to wait long for someone to let them into the block of flats as Calum noticed a young woman, maybe 25 years old, making her way down the stairs towards the main entrance where Calum and Sarah were standing.

The young woman was dressed in matching denim jeans and jacket and her hair was tied back tightly into a ponytail and she was carrying 2 large empty shopping bags. She was clearly going out on a shopping run.

The young woman reached the doors on the inside and pressed the button on the inside to open the doors.

There was a loud buzzing sound and the entrance doors in front of Calum and Sarah swung open.

The young woman exited the building and Calum and Sarah slipped in behind her before the doors could close.

Calum and Sarah looked around the ground floor of the flats they now found themselves in and found it to be a lot cleaner than they thought it was going to be. There was no smell of cheap alcohol or urine and there were no burnt pieces of aluminium foil or broken crack pipes or syringes anywhere.

This flat complex was clearly better looked after than other flat complexes of similar size in other deprived areas of Glasgow.

In the centre of the ground floor area of the flats there was a set of stairs leading up and an elevator on the right hand side.

"Should we take the elevator?" asked Calum.

"Absolutely." replied Sarah.

Both Calum and Sarah got into the elevator and Calum pressed the button for floor 7.

Less than a minute later the elevator doors slid open and Calum and Sarah were on the 7th floor of the flat complex.

In the centre of the floor there were concrete steps leading up and down to the other floors.

On the right was a door marked 13 with a large chrome door knocker positioned in the centre of the top third of the door.

On the left there was a standard white PVC door with the number 14 on the letterbox.

"This is the place." stated Calum pointing at the door.

Calum and Sarah walked over to the door.

"Here we go." said Calum as he chapped on the door loudly a few times.

Calum and Sarah waited for 30 seconds or so before Calum chapped the door again louder than before.

After another 30 seconds had passed Calum put his ear up against the door.

"I can hear the television," said Calum.

"He's definitely in." Calum continued.

Calum got down on his knees on front of the door and opened the letterbox and spoke into it loudly.

"Ricky. My name is Calum and I'm an acquaintance of Davie Dundas. I need to speak to you about something. If you let us in it'll only take us a couple of minutes." he said.

After speaking into the letterbox Calum stopped for a few seconds then sniffed deeply a couple of times.

Calum immediately let go of the letterbox flap and held his hand up to his mouth, almost vomiting.

"I know that smell" he said stepping away from the door.

"What is it?" asked Sarah.

Calum didn't answer Sarah he just took out his phone and quickly dialled a number.

"Hello. I want to report a dead body." said Calum into the phone.

3.00 pm. Tuesday. North West Glasgow

About 45 minutes after Calum made the phone call reporting a dead body both he and Sarah were sitting on the steps outside Ricky's front door being interviewed by a uniformed police officer.

Two paramedics wearing dust masks pushed a trolley with a black body bag on it past Calum, Sarah and the cop towards the elevator.

Sarah crossed herself as they walked past with the body in a body bag and on a trolley as she was a Catholic. She was not a devout Catholic as it had been many years since she last attended mass or confession but she still identified as being a Catholic.

One of the paramedics, the one at the front pushed the button for the elevator.

The officer interviewing Calum and Sarah was male and roughly the same age as Calum and he was just going over the statements both Calum and Sarah had given him.

The cop was reading information off a notebook he had previously jotted down all the relevant information on.

"So you arrived at this address at approximately 2.15pm looking to speak to Mr Sloane about something." the cop started.

"That's right." Calum said.

"You wanted to speak to him about an ongoing true crime piece you are both working on as you are both journalists." the cop continued.

"Yes" said Calum.

Sarah paused for a second before answering. She seemed distracted.

"Yes we are." said Sarah.

"And after you chapped the door and got no answer you spoke into the letterbox and that's when you smelled the odour of a dead body and called 999." the cop continued again.

"Yes." said Calum.

"I'm curious," the cop started.

"How did you know it was a dead body causing the stench?" he asked.

"When I was younger, when I was a teenager, I used to go on fishing trips with my friends often away in the middle of nowhere and a lot of the time we had to walk through farmer's fields to get to where we were going," started Calum taking a deep breath before continuing.

"Every once in a while we would come across a dead and decaying farm animal like a sheep or a cow. I remember the stench was awful and you could smell it from 50 yards away. It's a smell that you don't forget. The smell of rotting flesh." Calum explained.

"I see." said the cop.

Calum and Sarah briefly made eye contact and the expression on Calum's face told Sarah that the fishing story wasn't the truth. Calum knew the stench of death from somewhere else. Sarah didn't want to think about what the truth was.

The elevator doors opened and the 2 paramedics with the trolley entered the elevator and the doors closed behind them.

"Well whatever this ongoing crime story you're working on is, I can tell you that Mr Sloane has not been a part of it for at least 2 maybe as much as 3 weeks judging by the level of decomposition." said the cop.

"How did he die?" asked Sarah.

"We can't be sure until the post-mortem has been done but it looks like an overdose." replied the cop.
"We did he hear he was on smack." offered Calum.
"Well he was found sitting in his armchair in his living room with a cord wrapped around one of his arms with a discarded syringe lying on the floor and there was no sign of a struggle of any kind so I'd be very surprised if it turns out to be anything other than an accidental overdose." said the cop.
There was a pause for a few seconds where no one said anything then Calum spoke up.
"So are we free to go then?" Calum asked the cop.
"Of course." the cop replied.
Calum and Sarah both stood up then took a few steps towards the downwards stairs.
"Good luck with the crime story you're working on guys." said the cop as Calum and Sarah walked past him towards the downwards stairs.
"Thanks." said Calum.
"Thank you." said Sarah.
Calum and Sarah made their way down the stairs until they reached the ground level.
Calum pressed the button to open the main entrance door.
"Now what?" asked Sarah.
"Now we put your police researcher credentials to the test starting tomorrow. I'll take you home now and pick you up in the morning to take you to Maryhill police station." replied Calum.
"OK" said Sarah.

chapter four

Wednesday. 8.45am. South Glasgow

Sarah was putting the finishing touches to her makeup using the large wall mirror in the toilet of the flat she shared with Lorna.
Lorna had already left for work nearly half an hour ago so Sarah had the flat to herself and Calum would be picking her up at the bus stop across the road from where she lived at 9am and it was a 2 or maybe a 3 minute walk to the bus stop so she wasn't in a rush.
She was dressed smartly as always in a smart trouser suit with her hair tied up tightly in a bun.
After finishing her lip gloss in the mirror Sarah walked through to the kitchen to finish off a cup of coffee she had been drinking. She picked up the cup from the kitchen table and drank the last of the contents then looked at her watch. It was almost 8.55. Time to go.
Sarah placed the empty coffee cup into the sink and made her way to the front door. She opened the front door and noticed that it was raining slightly so she opened up a cupboard close to the front door and took out a small black umbrella to shelter her from the rain. It wasn't windy outside so the small umbrella would be sufficient.
Sarah made her way out of the flat, opened the umbrella, locked the flat door then made her way towards the bus stop pick up point.
The rain that was falling was a very light and very fine drizzle. The kind of rain that although it didn't look like

much to be bothered about given a chance would penetrate and soak anything it came into contact with.

As Sarah crossed the road towards the bus stop she noticed Calum's red Porsche waiting for her.

Sarah walked a little faster towards Calum's car and he opened up the passenger door when she got to it.

"Am I late?" asked Sarah getting into the passenger seat and collapsing her umbrella at the same time.

"No. I was early." replied Calum.

Sarah put the folded down umbrella at her feet and fastened her seatbelt.

Calum put the car in gear then drove off.

"Have you got your police ID?" asked Calum as he drove the car.

Sarah unfastened the top 2 buttons of her jacket, reached inside the jacket and pulled out her temporary police Scotland ID on a light chain around her neck.

"Got it right here." said Sarah.

Calum quickly glanced over at the ID badge. It was a white plastic credit card sized badge with some text and a Q.R. code on it.

"And that'll get you into all the police files you want?" asked Calum.

"As far as I know." replied Sarah.

There was a brief silent pause between Calum and Sarah before Calum spoke up.

"When you get in there and start searching for stuff I want you to concentrate on the first guy that got killed. Bob Campbell." said Calum.

"OK" replied Sarah.

"There's a reason he was the first guy targeted and there's a reason he was the only guy that was made to suffer."

Calum continued.

"I agree." said Sarah.

"He's the key to cracking this whole story. I can feel it. Once we find out what is special about him everything else will make sense so I want to know everything, and I do mean everything, the cops know about this Bob Campbell character. Did he do something? Was he involved in something? Was he a witness to something? Did he snitch on somebody?" said Calum.

"Got it." said Sarah.

After 20 minutes or so of driving Calum and Sarah arrived at their destination, Maryhill police station, an imposing 4 storey structure with a car park at the front of the building. Calum stopped his car outside the main entrance / exit door at the front of the building.

"Here we are," stated Calum as he stopped the car.

Sarah unfastened her seat belt and picked up her umbrella sitting between her feet.

"Call or text me the minute you find anything. I've got a meeting scheduled with the guy that runs my carpet and laminate flooring business for me but I'll finish it up early if you can find something for us to chase up." said Calum.

"I'll phone you as soon as I find anything." said Sarah.

"And Sarah," started Calum.

"Good luck." he continued.

"Thanks." Sarah replied.

Sarah got out the car and walked into the building.

As Sarah entered the building Calum drove off into the distance.

Inside the police station could be described as sparse as it was just a concrete corridor with wooden benches on the right hand side, a reception area behind some sliding glass windows on the left and large double doors at the far end of the corridor with a ID badge reader on the wall next to the handle.

Sarah walked over to the reception area windows and pressed the buzzer on the wall beside the windows.

A female police officer in full uniform approached the reception window from the other side and slid open the window.

"Can I help you?" asked the officer.

Sarah reached into her jacket and held out her police ID badge so the officer could see it.

"My name is Sarah Gibb. I'm a temporary civilian intelligence analyst and this is my first time here." stated Sarah.

The police officer squinted her eyes to look at Sarah's ID badge for a second then replied.

"Take a seat. Someone will see you shortly." said the officer.

Sarah walked over then sat down on one of the wooden benches on the other side of the corridor.

After 5 minutes or so had passed Sarah heard a loud buzzing sound coming from the door at the far end of the corridor and Ian stepped through the doorway and walked up to Sarah.

"Are you Sarah?" he asked.

"Yes." replied Sarah.

"I'm Ian. Ian Mckay. I handle IT for Police Scotland here at Maryhill station." said Ian as he reached out to shake Sarah's hand.

Sarah shook Ian's hand.

Ian was dressed sharply in a shirt and tie with an ID badge on a chain around his neck, he was in his early fifties and was over 6 feet tall. Probably closer to 6 feet 2 and was a fairly skinny guy with short grey hair. He didn't wear a wedding ring and had a slightly effeminate voice.

Sarah wondered if Ian was gay.
Possibly. But it's hard to tell these days.
Ian started to take a few steps back to the door at the far end of the corridor that he came from and he gestured for Sarah to follow him.

"If you just follow me I'll get your swipe badge activated and set you up with a user ID for the system. I'll also give you a quick orientation on how to use our system. All in all it should take about an hour." he said.
Sarah followed Ian to the door and Ian pressed his ID badge against the sensor and a green light appeared on the sensor, the door unlocked and Ian and Sarah walked through.

Wednesday. 10.45am. North Glasgow

Calum was sitting in a swivel chair in front of a desk in the office of Peter Swan, the guy that runs Calum's carpet and laminate flooring business for him.

Peter was sitting on the opposite side of the desk from Calum as this was his office.

Calum was dressed casually in jeans and a black shirt while Peter was dressed in his best suit as he knew the boss (Calum) was coming in to the workplace today.

Peter was in his mid-fifties, average build with short red hair and a moustache. He always wore a suit to work but today was a special day so he was wearing the best suit he had.

The office itself was fairly basic and was in fact just a large cupboard with a desk, a couple of chairs and a shelving set that ran along the wall of the entire length of the office from floor to ceiling.

The filing system was home to all the paperwork for the business. Mainly invoices from manufacturers and receipts for customers.

The business was set up in the 1970s so it pre-dated the widespread use of computers to store data and when Calum's dad bought over the company in the 2000s he felt there was no real need to fix something that wasn't broken so the paper-based system stayed in place.

Sitting on the desk between Calum and Peter was all the usual stuff you would expect to find on a manager's desk. A laptop, paperwork, in and out trays and framed pictures of Peter's grandchildren.

Peter knew Calum's dad Donald was a gangster when he bought over the business from the previous owners and didn't have a problem working for him. So when Donald died and the business ownership passed to his son Scott

Peter didn't have a problem working for him either. Then when ownership passed over to Calum after Scott's death Peter didn't have any issue working for him either.

Both Calum and Peter each had a folder full of computer printed documents open in front of them and they both were looking through all the information.

Peter was just finishing off talking Calum through the information in front of him.

"So as you can see our overall sales are up 8.2 percent compared to this time last year with sales expected to rise between 1.5 and 2 percent on top of that in the next financial quarter." stated Peter.

"That's excellent," replied Calum.

"I can see that. . . . ." Calum started to continue when his mobile phone started ringing.

Calum quickly took his phone out. It was Sarah calling.

"I need to take this." said Calum.

"I'll give you some privacy." said Peter making his way out the office door.

Calum answered his phone.

"Hello?" he said.

On the other end of the telephone call Sarah was sitting at a desk in a large open plan office area surrounded by other desks with various other men and women operating the computers in front of them.

"I think I've found something." Sarah said quietly trying not to be overheard.

"What have you found?" asked Calum.

"This time last year Bob Campbell was on remand at HMP Barlinnie." said Sarah quietly.

"Really? What was the charge?" asked Calum.

"He was in for grievous bodily harm. GBH. A really nasty case of torture committed against a senior citizen," started

Sarah.

"The case against him collapsed after the only witness against him, the victim, died of heart failure," she continued.

"Her name was Mary Macrae. She was 86 years old at the time of her death." Sarah continued again.

"How could the cops have missed this?" asked Calum.

"Well it was more than a year ago and it was expunged from his record when the case collapsed. I found this in the police intelligence files. They are kept separate from official criminal records." said Sarah.

Calum paused for a second before speaking again.

"Print off everything you can find on the crime and the victim and I'll pick you up in half an hour." said Calum.

"OK I'll see you then." said Sarah before ending the telephone call.

Calum stood up, put his phone back in his pocket and walked out the office door.

Calum met Peter outside the office.

"I need to go now but if you need to reach me for anything you've got my mobile number." said Calum quickly as he passed Peter.

"OK good to see you again Calum." said Peter.

"You too mate. You too." replied Calum.

Calum was trying to not get too excited but he was definitely pleased that they had found something that made Bob Campbell different from the other victims.

Wednesday. 11.15am. North West Glasgow

It had been almost exactly half an hour since Calum spoke to Sarah on the phone and he was driving his car through the Maryhill area of Glasgow towards Maryhill police station to meet Sarah.
It was still raining lightly outside and the sound of the car windscreen wipers were the only sound inside the car because Calum hadn't switched the radio on as he was deep in thought and he didn't want any distractions.
What did this new development mean?
Was Bob Campbell killed for committing this crime?
If Bob Campbell was killed for committing this crime, who did it and why were the other gang members being killed?
Were all of the CYT members now being targeted?
Calum thought about these questions over and over again until he reached his destination, Maryhill police station.
Calum turned his car into Maryhill police station car park. Sarah was standing in the exact spot Calum had dropped her off 2 hours previously with her umbrella in one hand and a plastic folder in the other. She had clearly gathered a lot of information.
Calum stopped the car to let Sarah in.
"The weather's not getting any better." commented Sarah as she entered the car placing her umbrella and her handbag at her feet and the folder on her lap.
"What have you found?" asked Calum.
"Quite a bit. Where do you want to start?" replied Sarah as she opened up the folder on her lap.
"Let's start with the victim. What have you got?" stated Calum.
Sarah looked through the printed documents in front of her.
"The victim was Mary Macrae. 86 years old. Widow. The only family I could find is her daughter who died in 1999

of a heroin overdose." Sarah read out from the documents. Another driver behind Calum peeped their car horn to get Calum to move.

"Have you got an address for her?" asked Calum as he started to drive off.

"Sure have," started Sarah as she looked through the paperwork again.

"82 Aprilfield Drive. Craiglen." she continued.

"Then that's where we'll start." said Calum as he drove his car out of the carpark and onwards towards Craiglen.

"She's been dead for nearly a year Calum. Somebody else will be living in the house now." said Sarah.

"True. But hopefully some of her neighbours will speak to us and tell us something that isn't in your files." said Calum.

"Maybe." said Sarah nodding her head in agreement.

A couple of minutes passed before Calum spoke up.

"Tell me about the crime." he said.

Sarah quickly looked through the paperwork on her lap.

"It was a really nasty case of torture," Sarah started.

"The victim was duct taped to a chair and had 3 of her fingers broken and she was also burned on her arms and legs with a clothes iron. Bob Campbell was after her pension and her savings. He tortured her to get her P.I.N. number for her debit card." she continued.

"Little bastard." Calum spat out.

"The ordeal went on for 3 days probably because the banks have a limit to how much money anyone can withdraw in a single day," said Sarah.

"She was discovered by one of her neighbours who had a key to her house and was worried about her because he hadn't seen her in a few days," Sarah continued.

"She was severely dehydrated and close to death. She nearly died Calum." Sarah continued again.

"So that probably explains why Bob Campbell was killed but we still have to find out why the other CYT members are being targeted." said Calum.

Wednesday. 11.45am. North Glasgow

Almost exactly half an hour after picking up Sarah at the police station Calum and Sarah were now driving through Aprilfield Drive in Craiglen.

Aprilfield Drive was a council street within Craiglen consisting of probably 120 semi-detached houses each with a small garden and constructed in a rectangle with odd numbered houses down one side of the road and evens down the other.

Calum was driving very slowly as both he and Sarah were counting door numbers.

"78, 80, 82 that's the house there." said Sarah pointing at number 82 in the street.

Calum mounted the path slightly to park his car up outside number 82. Both he and Sarah got out the car and made their way towards the front door of the house.

Calum pressed the doorbell.

After 20 seconds or so Michelle answered the door carrying a baby. She was in her early thirties and was dressed casually in tracksuit bottoms and T-shirt.

"Can I help you?" she asked.

Calum showed her one of his business cards.

"We're journalists and we'd like to speak to you about the woman that lived in this house before you moved in." he said.

"Never knew her," replied Michelle.

"I got allocated this house about 3 months after she died." Michelle continued.

"I see." said Calum.

"Do you know if she was friendly with any of the neighbours?" asked Sarah.

"Next door. Number 84," said Michelle pointing across the hedge that separated her house and the next door neighbour's.

"She was really close to Robbie and Moira Muir next door. Robbie had a key to her house. It was Robbie that found her when that wee bastard Campbell tied her up and tortured her and it was Robbie that found her after she died. When I first moved in I was still receiving mail from her son so I just passed it onto Robbie and Moira for safe keeping." explained Michelle.

"Her son?" asked Calum.

"Aye. Her son is in the army and he used to write to her all the time but Robbie and Moira will be able to tell you more about that. They've known him his entire life." said Michelle.

"OK thanks." said Calum.

Michelle closed the door and Calum and Sarah walked out of Michelle's property and into the next door neighbours. Number 84.

"I thought you said she only had a daughter." said Calum.

"According to the police records she had." replied Sarah.

Calum pressed the doorbell and Robbie answered the door quickly. He must have been close to the door when Calum pressed the doorbell.

"Hello." he said as he opened the door.

He was in his mid to late sixties and was dressed casually in trousers, a cardigan and slippers.

Calum showed him one of his business cards.

"We're journalists and we'd like to talk to you about Mary Macrae that used to live next door." stated Calum.

"What do you want to know?" asked Robbie.

"Who's at the door?" Moira said loudly from inside the house.

"A couple of journalists. They want to talk about Mary next door." said Robbie loudly over his shoulder so Moira could hear him.

"Well don't have them standing at the door. Invite them in." replied Moira.

"Come on in." said Robbie gesturing for Calum and Sarah to enter the house.

Calum stepped into Robbie and Moira's house closely followed by Sarah.

"In you go. First door on the right." said Robbie as he closed the front door behind them.

Calum and Sarah entered the living room area of Robbie and Moira's house where they were met by Moira who was sitting in a large padded chair next to the window.

Moira was in her mid to late sixties, she was wearing trousers, a cardigan and slippers similar to Robbie. She also had her hair in rollers.

The living room was fairly average for a married couple in their sixties. There was the chair Moira was sitting in, a matching chair on the other side of the room with a rolled up newspaper sitting on it probably left there by Robbie when he went to answer the door and a matching couch along the back wall of the room.

"C'mon in. Take a seat." said Moira pointing to the couch.

Calum and Sarah sat down on the couch. Robbie sat down on the spare chair.

"Can I get you something to drink?" asked Moira.

"A cup of tea or a cup of coffee?" she continued.

Calum looked at Sarah allowing her to answer first.

"No thank you." said Sarah.

"No thanks. I'm good." said Calum.

There was a brief pause before Calum spoke up.

"We appreciate you taking the trouble to talk to us. We'll only take up a few minutes of your time." started Calum.
"No it's no trouble at all. What would you like to know?" asked Moira.
"Anything you know about what happened to her." said Sarah.
"You want to know about what that wee laddie Campbell did to her?" asked Moira.
"Fucking junkie scumbag." spat out Robbie.
"Robbie! Watch your language when we have guests." said Moira.
"Well that's what he was." replied Robbie.
"You probably already know everything there is to know about it. Everybody in Craiglen knows about it." explained Moira.
"We only heard about it for the first time earlier today." said Calum.
"Well it had been 3 days since we had seen Mary which was unusual as we would normally see her pretty much every day at some point hanging out washing or sweeping the path and I noticed she hadn't been taking her milk delivery bottles into the house. So Robbie used the key she had gave him for emergencies and let himself into her house." explained Moira.
"I was worried she had fallen and hurt herself." said Robbie.
"That's right. We were worried she had fallen down and couldn't get up." continued Moira.
"So Robbie let himself in and that's when he found her tied up and gagged in the kitchen and he immediately called the police and an ambulance." Moira continued again.
"The paramedics told me that she was severely dehydrated and only hours away from death." said Robbie.

"So where was Bob Campbell when you let yourself into Mary's house?" asked Sarah.

"He was long gone. He probably got her cards and her financial details in the first hour or so of tying her up and torturing her. He just taped her up and left her to die." said Robbie.

"She was in hospital for about a week and then she got out. The police had already found and charged the guy that done it by the time she got out." said Moira.

"But that was just the start of her troubles." said Robbie.

"What do you mean?" asked Calum.

"What else happened?" asked Sarah.

"Bob Campbell's mates is what happened" started Robbie. "They started harassing her every chance they got trying to get her to drop the charges against Campbell," Robbie continued.

"First they started harassing her on the street when she was out doing her shopping. Then they smashed every window in her house on 3 separate occasions until the council fitted unbreakable Perspex windows. They put lit fireworks through her letterbox. And finally they kicked her door in twice in as many weeks and rushed into her house to hold knives to her throat and told her to drop the charges against Campbell." Robbie continued again.

"That's awful." said Sarah.

"I just wish I was 20 years younger and I didn't have a bad hip. I could have done something to help her but every time something happened all we could do is call the police and hope for the best." said Robbie.

"It might say on her death certificate that she died of heart failure but to those of us that know what she was put through we have no doubt that she was basically murdered." said Moira.

There was a brief silent pause before Calum spoke up again.

"Tell me about her son." he said.

"Brian is not really Mary's son he is in fact her grandson. The son of her daughter Angela who died because of drugs years and years ago when Brian was still a boy. Mary raised him as a son and she done a good job. He turned out to be a smashing young man." said Robbie.

"And handsome too," said Moira.

"He looks like that man in the gladiator film." Moira continued.

"Russell Crowe?" offered Sarah.

"That's the one." said Moira.

"Brian was one of those lucky people that always knew what they wanted to do in life and achieved it." said Robbie.

"And what's that?" asked Calum.

"Army. He always wanted to be in the army. As a child all he would play with was toy guns. No cars. No Lego. Just guns. So it was no surprise to anyone that knew him that he joined the Army straight after leaving school." said Robbie.

"Mary was really proud of him when he got accepted into the Army." said Moira.

"He didn't even know his mum had died until a couple of months ago when he got some leave time from the army and came home to visit Mary. He didn't even know about her funeral." Moira continued.

"The only way for them to communicate was by post." said Robbie.

"He was still writing letters to her for months after she died and it broke his heart in two when he found out what had happened to Mary. He had been working abroad and had no idea what had been happening." Robbie continued.

"When did he find out about what had happened?" asked Calum.

"About 2 months ago." said Moira.

"And things started getting interesting for us about 7 weeks ago." Calum said quietly to Sarah.

"He's popped in a couple of times since then just to say hello" said Moira.

"When was the last time you saw him?" asked Calum.

"Last Friday. The day before the cup final. He asked me if I knew anyone that had an abrasive wheel tool sharpener because he had something he needed sharpened so I sent him round to see my joiner mate Frankie. I asked Brian if he wanted to join mc for a few beers and to watch the football the following day. He said he'd like to but he had something important planned for that day." said Robbie.

Calum and Sarah looked at each other knowingly.

"Do you still have any of the letters he wrote to his mum?" asked Calum.

"I do aye." replied Robbie.

"Can I have a quick look at one of them?" asked Calum.

Robbie thought about it for a few seconds before answering.

"I'm sorry mate I can't let you read his letters. It just wouldn't be right." he answered.

"I don't want to read the contents. I just want to see the postmark." said Calum.

"I can do that." said Robbie as he stood up and walked out of the room to go and fetch one of Brian's letters.

Robbie returned less than a minute later with one of Brian's letters in his hand.

Robbie handed the letter to Calum.

Calum quickly took in all the info on the envelope and noticed there was 2 different postmarks. One of the postmarks was the standard Ministry of Defence (MOD) postmark and the other was just plain text saying SWAMPS.

Calum held the letter in one hand with his arm outstretched and quickly took his phone out and photographed the addressed side of the envelope.

Calum handed the envelope back to Robbie.

"Thanks Robbie. And thanks for talking to us. I think that'll be all we need to know from you." said Calum as he stood up followed by Sarah.

"It was nice meeting you both." said Sarah.

Calum handed Robbie one of his business cards.

"If Brian comes to your house again give him this." started Calum.

"Tell him I'd like to speak to him about what's been going on with the CYT." Calum continued.

"The CYT?" asked Robbie.

"He'll know what it's about." said Calum.

"OK. I'll show you out." said Robbie starting to walk towards the door.

Robbie escorted Calum and Sarah to the front door and out onto the path.

"Bye Robbie." said Calum as he walked out the door.

"Thanks for your time." said Sarah.

Both Calum and Sarah got back into Calum's car.

"Now it all makes sense." started Calum.

"Bob Campbell tortured and nearly killed Brian Macrae's mother, then gets his wee scumbag mates to terrorise her trying to get her in drop the charges. But the tough old bird wouldn't back down." he continued.

"But they take it too far and end up terrorising her to death." added Sarah.

"Brian was posted abroad at the time and Mary was the

only person that knew how to contact him. That's why it's taken nearly a year for him to come home." said Calum.
"And it explains why Bob Campbell was made to suffer and the others weren't. Brian tortured Bob partly as revenge for what he did to his mother and partly to find out the names of all the CYT members that were involved in terrorising her." said Sarah.
"The other CYT members that terrorised Mary were killed, were simply taken out in different ways, but all of them were killed up close and personal. Maybe he changed his methods with every kill to stop the cops looking into a serial killer or maybe he just enjoyed feeling their lives drain away in his hands." said Calum.
"As a trained soldier he's probably killed before and he probably knows the difference between killing someone at a distance and killing someone up close." said Sarah.
"That's right." said Calum.
There was a brief pause as both Calum and Sarah processed everything that had been said.
"Now what?" asked Sarah.
"Now we look into that SWAMPS. postmark on Brian's letters." said Calum.
"What do you think it means?" asked Sarah.
"At a guess I'd say it stood for South Western Army something or another. I really don't know. But I know a guy that will." said Calum as he started up the car.

Wednesday. 12.30pm. M8 motorway Eastbound

20 minutes after leaving Robbie and Moira in Craiglen Calum and Sarah were on the M8 motorway heading out of Glasgow and heading East.

Calum was driving the car while Sarah typed onto her phone in the passenger seat.

"There's nothing on Google about SWAMPS." she said.

"See if you can find some kind of postmarks database to search through," started Calum.

"Try and make it an international database. If he has been posted overseas he would probably have been using a foreign postal service." Calum continued.

"I'm on it." said Sarah engrossed in her phone.

A few minutes passed as Calum drove and Sarah searched the internet on her phone.

"So tell me about this guy we're going to meet." said Sarah.

"Donny?" started Calum.

"Donny McKay is a childhood friend of mine that served 15 years with the Royal Marine Commandos and he saw a lot of active combat in that time in Iraq and Afghanistan among other places.

There's not much that he doesn't know about the military. He finished up his time with the Marines a couple of years back and immediately bought a couple of acres and set up his paintball business in West Calder, West Lothian.

He picked West Calder because it's pretty close to being exactly halfway between Edinburgh and Glasgow and an easy commute from either city.

These days between the military contracts he has, the corporate team building exercises he supervises and the general customers that come his way he earns a pretty good living from the whole paintballing scene." said Calum.

"Cool." said Sarah.

Another 10 minutes passed before anyone spoke.

"Still can't find anything on SWAMPS on the internet." said Sarah.

"Don't worry about it. We'll be seeing Donny in the next 20 minutes," started Calum.

"He'll be able to tell us everything we want to know about whatever SWAMPS is." Calum continued.

Wednesday. 1.10pm. West Calder

After about another 15 minutes of motorway driving and a further 5 minutes of off motorway driving Calum and Sarah found themselves on a main road just South East of West Calder town.

Calum hadn't been here before so he didn't know exactly where it was. He had only exchanged messages with Donny on Facebook and Donny had told him his business was based South East of West Calder so it couldn't be far away from where they were now.

Every 100 metres or so there would be a small signpost pointing off the road they were on to smaller dirt track roads leading to various farms or businesses.

Eventually Calum found what he was looking for, a small signpost that read "Carnage paintball 300m" pointing off to the right of the main road.

"Here we go." said Calum as he turned the car onto the smaller dirt road.

Calum drove the car along the dirt track until he reached an area that was being used as a car park. There were 14 cars and 3 mini buses parked in the parking area.

Calum and Sarah got out of Calum's car and noticed another signpost that pointed to the right and read "reception area". They both followed the signpost to a large wooden hut that had most of one of the long sides cut out of it to form a very basic reception area.

Mags was sat inside the hut reading a newspaper. She immediately stood up when Calum and Sarah approached the hut.

"Can I help you?" she asked.

Mags was dressed in jeans and a red carnage paintball T-shirt and as she spoke Calum and Sarah both noticed her tongue stud that matched her nose stud.

"We're looking for Donny McKay." said Calum.

"OK." said Mags.

Mags took a few steps over to the side of the reception hut and took a 2-way radio walkie talkie off the wall and spoke into it.

"Donny McKay. Visitors at reception." she said.

"2 minutes." said Donny's voice on the radio.

Almost exactly 2 minutes later Donny arrived at reception. He was dressed in matching camouflaged trousers and jacket, he was wearing fingerless gloves and a full face protective mask. He quickly removed the mask as he approached Calum and Sarah.

"Calum. What the fuck?" he said as he shook Calum's hand and embraced Calum in a one arm man-hug.

"What the fuck are you doing through here?" he asked.

"Me and my colleague Sarah here came through to see if you could help us with something. We need some info." said Calum.

"Nice to meet you Sarah." said Donny nodding in her direction.

"And you too Donny." Sarah said back.

"Of course Calum anything you need" said Donny.

"Do you have somewhere we can talk?" asked Calum.

"Sure," Donny started as he walked away from the reception and into the woods.

"Follow me." he continued.

Calum and Sarah followed Donny into the woods to the designated rest area of the paintball business.

The rest area was pretty basic consisting of a roofed area perhaps 40 feet in length used for storing the participants' rucksacks with their food in them where they'd be safe from the rain and 6 large wooden benches for the participants to sit on while they ate their food.

The entire area was surrounded by 10 feet high green tightknit plastic fishnet mesh to protect the resting participants from stray paintball pellets.

Donny walked over to the roofed area, opened up a rucksack and took out a bottle of water. He unscrewed the lid as he walked back over towards Calum and sat down on one of the wooden benches. Calum and Sarah stood in front of him.

"It's been a long time Calum." Donny said as he took a swig from the bottle.

"Too long." replied Calum.

"What can I help you with?" he asked.

"We're interested in finding a military guy and we know he's been sending letters with the postmark SWAMPS. as well as the regular MOD postmark on it. We were wondering what the SWAMPS. postmark means. We can't find anything about it anywhere on the internet." said Calum.

Calum showed Donny the photograph on his phone of the letter he photographed in Robbie and Moira's home.

Donny took another swig from his water bottle.

"I was thinking that it stands for South Western Army something or another but you'll know better than me." Calum continued.

"No you are way off target mate." said Donny.

"What is then? What does it mean?" inquired Calum.

"It goes back to the first year of the war in Afghanistan. The MOD found that it was much better for the mental health of their special forces troops if they had fairly regular contact with their friends and family. Letters mostly. But the existing MOD postal service wasn't up to the task of locating the troops at any given time which is easy to understand as the nature of the special forces operations meant they were relocating all the time. A few days here then a few days there and so on. It would be hard for anyone to keep track," said Donny as he took another swig from his water bottle.

"The solution they came up with was to form a separate postal service within the existing M.O.D. postal service. They called it the Specialist Warfare Advanced Military Postal Service, the SWAMPS. or the Swamp Service for short."

Calum and Sarah looked at each other and Donny swigged from his water bottle.

"If the guy you are looking for has been using the swamp service then he's either SAS or SBS. Special Air Service or Special Boat Service depending on whether he's Army or Navy." explained Donny.

"Army," said Calum.

"The guy we're looking for is Army." Calum continued.

"Well he'll be SAS then" said Donny.

There was a brief pause before anyone spoke up.

"I know you are working as a journalist now so I'm going to take a guess and say that you are interested in this guy because he's went off the rails and done something he probably shouldn't." said Donny.

"That's an understatement." said Sarah.

"I've only got one word of advice for you if you are going to fuck with this guy and that word is don't. Don't fuck with this guy. Don't open up that can of worms. You need to understand that for these guys killing someone is as easy as blowing out a candle and if he's went off the rails there's no telling how he might react to someone getting in his way. You don't want to be in a position where this guy sees you as a threat." explained Donny.

"He won't. It won't come to that." said Calum.

Calum reached his hand out to shake hands with Donny.

"It was good to see you again." said Calum.

Donny stood up, shook Calum's hand and gave him a one armed man-hug.

"You too mate. You too." responded Donny.

Calum and Sarah started to walk away.

"Don't be a stranger." Donny said loudly.

Calum gave Donny the thumbs up signal as he and Sarah walked back towards the car park area.

"Now what do we do?" asked Sarah.

"Now we go and speak to the CYT again to find out who else was involved in terrorising Mary Macrae. We need to find out who else is on Brian's kill list." said Calum.

Wednesday. 2.40pm. North Glasgow.

Calum and Sarah were standing outside the block of flats where they met with Razzy and some of the CYT the day before.

Calum pressed the intercom button for flat 112.

The intercom beeped for a few seconds before someone answered.

"Hello?" said a voice over the intercom.

"It's Calum McCulkin here I need to speak to Razzy." said Calum into the intercom.

"Razzy's not here." said the voice over the intercom.

"Well phone him and tell him to get his arse here. Tell him it's a matter of life and death." said Calum into the intercom system.

"Wait a minute." said the voice over the intercom.

Calum and Sarah paused for a minute or so waiting for a reply over the intercom.

"Are you still there?" said the voice on the intercom.

"We're here." said Calum back into the intercom.

"Razzy says he'll be here in about 20 minutes if you try again then." said the voice on the intercom.

"OK I'll be back in 20 minutes." said Calum into the intercom.

Calum and Sarah walked away from the flat entrance, down a flight of steps and along the road towards where Calum had parked his car.

Calum was muttering to himself loud enough for Sarah to hear what he was saying.

"Fucking granny bashers," he said.

"This Brian Macrae character deserves a medal for getting rid of them. Not prison." he continued.

Calum unlocked the car with his remote key and both he and Sarah got in.

"I don't even know why we're here. We shouldn't be warning them. We shouldn't be trying to save their lives. We should just let Brian do whatever the fuck he wants to do to them. They deserve it." Calum said out loud.

"If you find out someone's life is in danger you should always warn them." offered Sarah.

"Even if they are a piece of shit granny basher?" asked Calum.

"Even if they are a piece of shit granny basher." replied Sarah.

Calum was genuinely angry with these guys as granny bashers were pretty much at the bottom of the food chain in his world. They were the scum of the Earth and Calum agreed with Moira when she said that despite Mary's death certificate stating that she died of natural causes she had in fact been murdered by these scumbags.

Approximately 25 minutes later a dark blue Vauxhall Astra with a lowered suspension, tinted windows and a big bore exhaust slowly drove past and stopped a little way along the road.

It was a boy racer car meaning it was a modified version of a fairly average car with a heavy duty sound system because all the time it was in view the boom boom boom of a techno track being played loudly could be heard all the way along the street.

Calum and Sarah watched the car doors open and Razzy, Tony and Welshy get out the car and walk towards the flat.

"Here we go." said Calum opening up his door and getting out the car followed by Sarah who did the same.

Calum and Sarah walked along the path until they reached the small flight of concrete steps that lead up to the block of flats Razzy was in.

Calum and Sarah reached the flats they were at 25 minutes ago looking for Razzy.

Calum was ready to press the intercom system when Sarah put her hand across the button so Calum couldn't press it.

"You need to keep your cool up here," she started.

"I know you don't like these guys and I know you hate what they did to Mary Macrae." she continued.

"When you're talking about how I feel about what they did to Mary Macrae the word hate is an understatement." said Calum as he gently pushed Sarah's hand aside and pressed the intercom button.

"Hello?" said the same voice as before over the intercom system.

"It's Calum McCulkin. I'm here to speak to Razzy. I know he's here." said Calum into the intercom.

There was a loud buzzing sound and the sound of the door unlocking.

Calum and Sarah stepped into the block of flats and started to walk up the concrete staircase towards flat 112.

Less than a minute later Calum and Sarah were at the door to flat 112 and Calum pressed the doorbell.

A few seconds later Welshy opened the door dressed in the usual attire, a white Lacoste tracksuit and a Burberry pattern skip cap and he was swigging from a bottle of Buckfast.

"C'mon in." he said to Calum and Sarah.

Calum and Sarah entered the flat to be greeted by Razzy sitting on the couch with Tony and Mick, each sitting on one of the chairs on either side of the glass table in front of the couch Razzy was on.

Razzy, Tony and Mick were all dressed pretty much the same in tracksuits, trainers and skip caps.

The entire flat stank of alcohol and weed. Razzy was also drinking from a bottle of Buckfast.

Calum and Sarah stood in the centre of the room facing Razzy on the couch.

"Well well well," said Razzy.

"Calum McCulkin. The intrepid reporter and his sidekick. I'm sorry I forgot your name." he continued.

"Sarah. My name is Sarah." said Sarah.

"Ah that's right. Sarah. His sidekick Sarah." said Razzy.

Razzy took a swig from his Buckfast bottle.

"So what can I do for you Calum? I hear you want to speak to me about a matter of life and death." said Razzy.

"That's right," said Calum pausing for a few seconds before continuing.

"We've put all the pieces together." said Calum.

"The pieces of what?" asked Razzy.

"The puzzle. The puzzle of why your gang members have been getting murdered recently." stated Calum.

"And why would that be?" asked Razzy.

"Punishment. Punishment and revenge." said Calum.

"Punishment and revenge for what?" asked Razzy.

Calum could tell Razzy knew exactly what he was taking about and he didn't like Razzy playing dumb with him.

"Punishment and revenge for the torture and subsequent murder of a senior citizen in Aprilfield Drive a year and a bit ago." said Calum as he was totally convinced that what happened to Mary Macrae was murder.

"Murder?" said Razzy playfully.

"Aye, murder," started Calum starting to get angry.

"No-one was ever charged with murder over it but it was definitely murder. She was terrorised to death." Calum continued.

"I don't know anything about a murder in Aprilfield Drive

last year but I do remember hearing about some old cow in Aprilfield Drive having a heart attack and dying. Maybe that's who you're talking about." said Razzy smiling.

"She wasn't an old cow." said Calum barely able to contain his growing anger with Razzy.

Calum inhaled then exhaled deeply before continuing.

"I want to know the name of everybody that was involved in the terrorising of Mary Macrae." he said as calmly as he could.

Razzy shook his head a few times before answering.

"Never going to happen," he said.

"In the CYT we don't snitch on our mates. Even when they're dead." he continued.

"Even when it means saving their lives?" asked Calum.

There was a brief pause before Razzy spoke up.

"It's none of your business. You should just leave it alone. As far as I'm concerned the old cow shouldn't have snitched in the first place. She deserved everything that happened to her." said Razzy smiling.

Calum violently kicked over the glass table in front of him sending a bottle of Buckfast and 2 overflowing ashtrays over Razzy. Then he immediately reached over and grabbed Razzy by the upper chest area and picked him up until Razzy was standing on his tiptoes.

"Listen to me you little rat bastard, everybody involved in terrorising Mary Macrae is going to fucking die and I might be the only guy that can stop it from happening so I suggest you start helping me." spat out Calum.

Welshy, Tony and Mick all produced knives and held them up to Calum's face and throat. Welshy produced a 6 inch lock knife, Tony produced a butterfly knife and Mick produced a box cutter knife.

There was a tense few seconds of silence before Razzy spoke up again.

"Put the blades away boys. It's OK." he said to his gang mates who very slowly complied with his wishes and put the knives away.

"Take your fucking hands off me McCulkin." Razzy spat out.

Calum waited a few seconds then let go of Razzy and took a few steps back

Razzy immediately dusted himself off.

"Out of respect for your family name I'll let you off with that just once," he started.

"But if you ever raise your hand to me again I'll have one of my boys here rip you from your earhole to your arsehole". he continued.

"You little . . ." said Calum taking a step closer to Razzy but Sarah stepped in front of him.

"Let's go. He's not going to help. Nothing good is going to come out of this situation." said Sarah.

"You should do what the bitch says McCulkin. You should leave right now before something bad happens to you. To both of you." said Razzy.

Calum took a deep breath before replying to Sarah.

"You're right. We should go. There's nothing I can do if the guy won't work with me." he said.

Calum and Sarah started walking towards the door when Razzy called out.

"And one more thing McCulkin." Razzy started.

Calum stopped walking for a second to hear what Razzy had to say.

"And what's that?" Calum asked.

"Don't ever some back. Ever." said Razzy.

Calum shook his head before replying.

"I just hope for your sake you weren't involved in this Razzy." said a Calum before walking through the door being held open by Tony.

Two minutes later Calum and Sarah were walking the 50 yards or so to Calum's parked car when Tony came running up behind them.

"Mate. Mate." he shouted as he ran up to them.

Calum spun around on the spot expecting some kind of confrontation.

"What is it?" Calum asked.

"I can give you the name of one of the guys you are looking for," said Tony while trying to regain his breath as he was seriously out of shape.

"He's my cousin. Mark Sneddon. He gets called Sned. He was one of the guys that was harassing that old woman in Aprilfield Drive last year. If his life's in danger he needs to know." said Tony.

"And how do I get hold of Sned?" asked Calum.

"He's in the clink. He's doing a five stretch in Barlinnie for armed robbery." explained Tony.

Calum and Sarah looked at each other.

"OK thanks we'll look into it." said Calum opening up the car doors with the remote key.

"Tell him Tony says he should speak to you. It's in his best interests.'" said Tony as he turned to walk back to the flats.

Calum and Sarah got into Calum's car.

"That could've went better up there" said Sarah.

"Aye it could've." replied Calum.

"So what now then?" asked Sarah.

"Now we call it a day and head home. I'll take you to the police station tomorrow morning so you can see what you can find on Brian Macrae and this piece of shit Mark Sneddon and I'll make some phone calls to see if we can

get an appointment to go and visit Sneddon in jail as soon as possible." said Calum.
"OK." said Sarah.

Wednesday. 8.30pm. West end of Glasgow.

Calum opened the door and walked into his gym ready for his nightly workout. He was dressed in dark tracksuit bottoms and a loose fitting white T-shirt ready to do some sweating.

Firstly, he stepped onto the running machine treadmill and switched it on. Slowly at first but speeding it up every few seconds until he was running almost as fast as he could.

As he got into the running part of his workout questions about the whole situation plagued him.

What was he going to do now that he knew Sned was on Brian's hit list?

Would he just warn Sned or would he get the cops involved to try and keep him safe?

Did he want to get the cops involved at all?

Did the guys on Brian's hit list deserve what was happening to them?

Did he even want to see Brian prosecuted at all for what he had been doing?

These questions rattled around in Calum's head all the way through his workout. Through the running machine, through the abs board and through the butterfly weights bench.

chapter five

8.55am. Thursday. South Glasgow.

It was another rainy Thursday morning in the Shawlands area of South Glasgow and Calum had parked his car at the bus stop across the road from Sarah's flat.
The rain that fell onto Calum's car windscreen was continually being wiped away every few seconds by the windscreen wipers set to intermittently wipe the front window.
Calum had both hands on the steering wheel and he was tapping the steering wheel quickly with both his thumbs.
He turned his right arm so he could see his watch.
It was 8.55am.
Calum noticed Sarah on his right hand side crossing the road. She was smartly dressed as always and holding onto a black umbrella to shelter her from the rain.
Sarah opened up the passenger side door on Calum's car and got in.
"Have you been waiting here long?" she asked as she collapsed her umbrella down to a smaller size and fastened her seat belt.
"Just got here." replied Calum as he put the car in gear and started to drive away.
"So you want me to find everything I can about Mark Sneddon and Brian Macrae?" asked Sarah.
"That's right." said Calum.
"You rake through the police records to see what you can find and I'll try to get us a visit for later today to speak to

this scumbag Sned." Calum continued.

"OK." said Sarah.

"Visits to the prison usually need to be booked a few days in advance but I'm pretty sure I can get us in today." said Calum.

"I'll print off hard copies of everything I find for us to look over before we go to the prison." said Sarah.

"Aye. Do that." said Calum.

"Visiting times are from 2 until 3 and from 3 until 4 so I'll come and pick you up at 1 o'clock. That'll give you about 3 and a half hours to search the police system for info." Calum continued.

"That should be plenty of time." said Sarah nodding her head in agreement as she spoke.

Approximately 25 minutes later Calum stopped his car outside the main entrance to Maryhill police station and Sarah got out the car.

"I'll see you at 1 o'clock." said Calum as Sarah started to close the car door.

"OK I'll see you then." replied Sarah as she closed the car door.

Sarah quickly walked up the half dozen or so steps outside Maryhill police station then entered the building via the main entrance. She calmly walked into the main reception corridor, flashing her swipe ID badge at the police officer behind the window as she passed and on to the access door at the far end of the corridor.

Sarah walked up to the access door at the far end of the reception corridor and tapped her swipe ID badge on the sensor at the side of the door.

The little light on the card sensor turned from red to green and the door unlocked. Sarah walked through the doorway and into the heart of the police station.

1pm. Thursday. North West Glasgow

Calum was sitting in his car outside the main entrance to Maryhill police station. He was sitting in almost complete silence with no radio on and the only sound in the car was his right index finger tapping on the steering wheel almost in time with the raindrops falling onto the windscreen.
Calum looked at his watch. It was exactly 1pm.
Sarah exited from the police station via the main entrance doors and made her way to Calum's car. She was holding her umbrella in her right hand and some cardboard folders in her left.
Calum reached over and opened up the door for Sarah. Sarah got into the car and immediately folded down her umbrella and placed it at her feet.
"Did you find much?" asked Calum as he started to drive away.
"Sure did." said Sarah.
"What did you find?" asked Calum.
"Who do you want to know about? Sneddon or Macrae?" answered Sarah.
Calum paused for a few seconds before answering Sarah.
"Tell me about Sneddon." said Calum.
Sarah quickly opened up one of the cardboard folders she was carrying and took out some paper computer print offs.
"Born Mark Anthony Sneddon. Aged twenty four. Mother is Tracy Sneddon. Father unknown. He's a naughty boy and he's been in and out of prisons and young offender institutions regularly since he was fourteen. Assault, serious assault, possession of a knife and a few drug possession charges. In fact, in the last ten years he's been locked up almost exactly the same amount of time he's been free." said Sarah.
"OK tell me about Macrae." said Calum.

Sarah opened up the other folder she was carrying and started to read from it.

"As far as I can tell Brian Macrae doesn't have any criminal record at all," Sarah started.

"But that doesn't mean I couldn't find anything on him." Sarah continued.

"What did you find?" asked Calum.

"The SAS are based in Hereford, England right?" said Sarah.

"Right." replied Calum.

"So I did a driving license search for Brian Macrae for all of Herefordshire and I got three hits. One guy is 73." said Sarah.

"Too old." said Calum.

"Another is 21." said Sarah.

"Too young." said Calum.

"And the third hit was for a guy aged 34." said Sarah.

"Could be our guy." said Calum.

"So next I printed off a copy of his driving license," said Sarah rummaging through the paperwork in front of her.

"And guess what?" asked Sarah.

"He does look like Russell Crowe in Gladiator," said Sarah holding up a piece of paper so Calum could see.

"Just like Moira said." Sarah continued.

"What else have you got on Macrae?" asked Calum.

"As far as I can tell he's never been charged with anything ever. He's as clean as a whistle. The only thing I could find on Macrae is the car he drives. I did a quick insurance check on any vehicles registered to his home address and found that he drives a silver 2018 registration Volkswagen Golf diesel." said Sarah.

"That's some good work you've done today." said Calum.

"Thanks." said Sarah.

There was a short pause in the conversation before Sarah spoke up.
"How did you get on arranging an appointment for us to go and speak to Sneddon in prison?"
"We've got an appointment for half past three," said Calum.
"We'll go to my place to study the information you've uncovered then we'll visit this piece of shit Sneddon." Calum continued.

1.30pm. Thursday. West Glasgow.

Calum and Sarah had just entered Calum's house and had made their way to the kitchen, a large and fully equipped open-plan futuristic white marble effect area centred around a huge aluminium effect American style fridge freezer with a large island in the middle of the room.
They had an hour to kill before they had to leave to get to their appointment at the prison.
Sarah placed the two cardboard folders she was carrying down onto the kitchen island while Calum opened up the fridge door.
"Do you want something to drink?" he asked Sarah.
"What have you got?" replied Sarah.
"Orange juice, mineral water, Irn Bru, tea or coffee." said Calum.
"I'll have a water please." replied Sarah.
Calum reached into the fridge and took out two bottles of water. One for him and one for Sarah. Calum handed Sarah one of the bottles of water, unscrewed the lid on his bottle and took a big swig.
"I don't think there's much use going over the info you've gathered on Macrae because there's nothing interesting there. Like you said he's as clean as a whistle." said Calum.
"OK so we'll concentrate on Sneddon." said Sarah as she opened up the folder she had containing all the info she had gathered on Sneddon.
Sarah handed half the paperwork to Calum.
Calum's eyes quickly scanned through the top document of the pile of documents Sarah had just handed him.
"It says here he was first locked up at fourteen years old for possession of an offensive weapon, a lock knife. He got sentenced to nine months in a children's secure unit and he served four and a half months then he was released." said

Calum.

"In less than a year he was locked up again for serious assault," started Sarah.

"This time he got eighteen months and he served nine months. He served the first three months in a children's secure unit because he was still under sixteen then the following six months in the young offenders' institution at Polmont." Sarah continued.

"Nine months later he was up in court again. This time for possession with intent to supply a controlled substance. Weed," started Calum.

"He pleaded guilty and was sentenced to three years. He served eighteen months in the young offenders' institution and was released again." Calum continued.

"His list of convictions just goes on and on. Do you really want to go through all of it?" asked Sarah.

"No. You're right," started Calum.

"We'll just skip to his latest conviction." Calum continued. Sarah quickly looked through the paperwork in front of her.

"Got it." she proclaimed as she held a piece of paper out in front of her and quickly scanned through the document for information.

"He was jailed in January of this year for armed robbery. He robbed a corner shop brandishing a hunting knife. He was caught on CCTV. in the shop. He didn't even bother to wear a mask." said Sarah.

"Fucking idiot." said Calum.

"He got away with £120 and got five years for his trouble." Sarah continued as she handed the document over to Calum.

"Five years for stealing £120. That's not even £25 for every year he got sentenced to." said Calum quietly as he read the document.

"He tried to plead not guilty by means of diminished responsibility due to intoxication. He claimed he blacked out while full of alcohol and benzodiazepines and didn't know anything about the robbery until the police kicked his door in the following day." said Sarah.

"He might be telling the truth. It wouldn't be the first time I've heard of someone blacking out and committing a violent crime because of a belly full of booze and downers." said Calum.

"Now what?" asked Sarah.

"Now we get ready to visit Sned," said Calum.

"You'll need either a passport or a photographic driving license plus a utility bill in your name to get into the visiting area." Calum continued.

"I've got a passport and a gas bill at home." said Sarah.

"That'll do," said Calum.

"We'll stop off at your place on the way to the prison." Calum continued.

3.00pm. Thursday. North East Glasgow

Calum parked his car in the visitor's carpark outside Barlinnie prison in the Riddrie area in North East Glasgow. The carpark was fairly small with enough parking spaces for around fifty cars in total and Calum's Porsche did not look out of place amongst some of the cars parked here. The visitor's car park had quite a few expensive high performance sports cars in it. Mostly Japanese or German sports cars like sporty Subarus, Mitsubishis, Audis, BMWs or Mercedes all driven by beautiful young women. Girlfriends and partners of drug dealer inmates.

All of the young women visitors had a similar look. They were all spray tan orange and they were all wearing huge fake eyelashes and fingernails.

There was a time, it seems like an eternity ago, where prison populations would be made up of a mixture of all kinds of criminals. Bank robbers, cat burglars, safe crackers etc. but these days it's almost all about drugs. The majority of prisoners nowadays are either drug dealers or drug addicts and since drug addicts generally don't own nice cars there is a good chance anyone visiting the prison in a nice car is there to visit a drug dealer.
Calum and Sarah closed their car doors and started walking towards the main entrance.
From the outside the prison looked sleek and modern with nice brickwork and a glass enclosed reception area but away from the reception area and into the accommodation halls the structure was far from modern.
The five accommodation halls in H.M.P. Barlinnie were built in stages during the Victorian period with the first hall being built in 1882 and the most recent in 1897 so even the most modern accommodation hall was not modern at all.
As they reached the visitors entrance Calum held the heavy reinforced glass door open for Sarah.
"Thanks." said Sarah.
As Calum and Sarah entered the reception area they were immediately approached by Supervising Prison Officer Bruce McLaren, an old acquaintance of Calum's.
Calum knew Bruce because Bruce used to work for Calum's dad back when Calum's dad had business interests in the security industry. Mostly building site security.
Bruce was a good hire for Calum's Dad because he was known as a straight arrow as he had never made a pound from anything illegal and he had never spent an hour in police custody never mind charged or convicted for anything.
The fact that Bruce was six foot four, weighed a muscly

twenty stone and could handle himself in a fight was just a bonus for Calum's dad as the more important issue was his lack of a criminal record.

After Calum's dad ended his interests in the security industry around 2005 Bruce found work with similar groups in the city before deciding to join the Scottish Prison Service ten years ago where he had built a reputation among the staff and the prisoners as being firm but fair in the job.

Bruce reached out to Calum and shook his hand.

"Good to see you again Calum." said Bruce.

"Good to see you too mate. Thanks for getting me a visit arranged at such short notice." replied Calum.

"Not a problem." said Bruce.

"Bruce this is my workmate Sarah." Calum continued.

"Hello Sarah." said Bruce.

"Nice to meet you Bruce." replied Sarah.

Bruce started to walk Calum and Sarah across the reception area towards the visitor's check in area where another officer, Ian, was standing.

"If you just make your way to the visitor's primary check-in area my colleague Ian here will tell you what to do." said Bruce as Ian stepped towards Calum and Sarah.

The visitor's primary check-in area consisted of a 3 metre long, chest height desk with a counter on top of and a prison officer operating a computer on the other side.

"Name?" asked the officer behind the desk.

"Calum McCulkin." said Calum.

"Name of inmate?" asked the officer as he typed on the computer.

"Mark Sneddon." said Calum.

Identification?" asked the officer.

Calum reached into his inside jacket pocket, pulled out his

passport and a utility bill from his house and placed them on the desk in front of the prison officer.

The prison officer picked both of the items up, quickly scanned through the utility bill with his eyes then opened up the passport and put it under an ultra-violet light on his desk.

After a few seconds the prison officer had processed Calum's identification and handed them both back.

"Next." said the officer from behind the desk.

Sarah stepped forward.

"Name?" asked the officer.

"Sarah Gibb." said Sarah.

"Name of inmate?" asked the officer.

"Mark Sneddon." said Sarah.

"Identification?" asked the officer.

Sarah reached into her handbag and took out her passport and a utility bill from her home and placed it on the table in front of the prison officer.

The officer took the items and quickly looked through the utility bill then opened up the passport and placed it under the ultra-violet scanner.

After a few seconds the prison officer had processed Sarah's identification and handed them both back.

"If you both follow me I'll take you to your locker area to keep your valuables while you are having your visit." said Ian as he walked Calum and Sarah across to the other side of the reception hall to the locker room.

A few seconds later Calum, Sarah and Ian reached the visitor's locker room, a rectangular hallway with grey metal lockers down both sides. There were probably sixty lockers in total and every one of them had a small key in the door.

"If you put your valuables into a locker I'll walk you

through to the security check area and then the visitors waiting area before your visit starts." said Ian.

Calum and Sarah quickly put all their valuables into their respective lockers. Mobile phones, keys, wallet/purse and Sarah's handbag.

Both Calum and Sarah took the keys out of their lockers ready to move onto the security check area.

"Are you both ready?" asked Ian.

"Aye." said Calum.

"Yes." said Sarah.

"OK let's go." said Ian.

Ian quickly lead Calum and Sarah out of the locker area and to a set of double doors on the left to the security check in area.

The visitor's security check area consisted of a waist high conveyer belt with an x-ray scanner in the middle of it manned by a prison officer, not unlike the similar scanners you would find in an airport, a walk-through metal scanner doorway, another officer with a metal detecting wand on the other side of the doorway and another officer with a Spaniel on a leash to sniff all visitors to the prison.

All of the prison officers were dressed exactly the same with black trousers, a white shirt and a black tie.

The black ties the prison officers were all wearing were the clip-on variety instead tied around the neck because the round the neck ties were a strangulation hazard if the officer wearing it got into a violent struggle with an inmate.

All of the officers also wore a utility belt with separate pouches holding handcuffs, telescopic metal truncheon and pepper spray. They all also carried a two way radio clipped to their belts.

"If you take a tray each and put any metallic objects you might still be carrying into it we can get started." said Ian pointing towards a pile of grey plastic trays at the nearside of the conveyer belt.

Neither Calum nor Sarah had any metallic objects left on them after the locker room.

"I don't have any metallic objects on me." said Calum.

"Me neither." said Sarah.

Ian nodded towards the officer operating the conveyer belt scanner to let her know Calum and Sarah were OK to move onto the next stage.

"Now if you just step through the doorway." Ian said to Calum.

Calum stepped through the metal detecting doorway and the doorway made a loud beeping sound. Calum still had something metallic on him.

The officer with the metal detecting wand stepped over to Calum.

"Spread your arms out please." said the officer.

Calum complied and spread his arms out on either side of him while the prison officer scanned him with the wand around both arms then the chest then the crutch. That's when the wand detected something.

"It'll be the buttons on my trousers." said Calum.

The prison officer with the wand glanced over at Bruce and Bruce nodded to signal it was OK to let Calum through.

Next up was the sniffer dog test. The officer with the dog pointed at a large yellow painted circle on the floor.

"Stand over there mate." said the officer with the dog.

Calum stepped over to the circle and waited to be sniffed. The officer with the dog stepped over to Calum and quickly walked around him with the dog in a clockwise direction with the dog sniffing at Calum and its tail wagging all the time.

After a few seconds the officer and the dog stepped back to

the spot they were stood at before checking Calum.
Sarah stepped through the metal detecting doorway and the door didn't go off. She had no metallic objects on her at this point so she didn't need to be scanned again with the wand.

"Stand on the yellow dot please." the officer with the dog said to Sarah.

Sarah took the few steps over to the yellow circle on the floor and stood still to be sniffed at.

The officer with the dog quickly walked around Sarah with the dog sniffing at her all the time before returning back to his starting position.

Ian approached Calum and Sarah.

"We're heading through here on the right." Ian continued gesturing for Calum and Sarah to go through a doorway on their right hand side.

Calum and Sarah walked through the doorway and into the visitor's waiting area.

"Someone will come and get you when the inmate you are visiting is ready for you." said Ian as he walked away.

The visitor's waiting area consisted of five rows of ten seats made up of aluminium frames running the length of each individual row. The aluminium frames had padding attached to create a sitting area and the frames were bolted into the ground to prevent them from being picked up and used as weapons in the event of a fight breaking out between visitors.

Calum and Sarah sat down on a seat each at the front of the room. There were six other visitors in the visiting room already.

Two of them were young women in their twenties caked in makeup with false eyelashes and spray on tans sitting talking quietly together at the far end of the waiting room.

Probably the girlfriends or partners of drug dealer inmates. In the middle of the room sat a couple, a man and a woman, both in their fifties talking together. Probably the parents of an inmate.
Close to the couple in the centre of the room a woman sat alone. She was fiftyish and plainly dressed. Possibly the mother of an inmate or possibly the partner of an inmate. On the left hand side of the entrance door sat a schemie not unlike Razzy and the other CYT schemies Calum and Sarah met the other day in Craiglen.
The schemie in the waiting room was dressed the way they were always dressed. Tracksuit, trainers and skip cap. He was obviously in to visit one of his schemie mates that was doing time.
After a few minutes the entrance door opened and a male prison officer stepped into the waiting room.
"Robert McLeary." said the officer loud enough for everyone to hear.

One of the young women at the far end of the waiting room stood up and started to walk towards the male prison officer.
The prison officer and the young woman both walked through the doorway and on to the main visiting area.
After another few minutes the same male prison officer stepped through the doorway.
"Steven Courtney." he said loud enough for everyone to hear.
The schemie sitting next to the entrance door stood up.
"That'll be for me mate." said the schemie.
The prison officer and the schemie both walked through the doorway and on to the main visiting area.
Over the next 10 or 15 minutes the same male prison officer came into the room, said the name of a male

prisoner out loud then lead someone from the waiting room to the visiting area several times. Other visitors also entered the waiting room. A girl in her late teens with a baby, a couple of women in their fifties and another schemie. Eventually it was Calum and Sarah's turn.

The male prison officer stepped through the doorway.

"Mark Sneddon." he said loudly.

"That's us. Let's go." said Calum as he stood up and walked towards the prison officer standing in the doorway followed closely by Sarah.

The male prison officer walked Calum and Sarah along a short corridor that opened out into fairly large hall used for visits. The hall was probably fifty feet by one hundred feet and it had ten large circular tables for the visitors and the inmates to sit at. The tables were probably six feet each in diameter and had plastic chairs around all of them.

At this point seven of the ten tables were in use with inmates getting visits from friends and family. The inmates were all dressed the same in prison issue jogging trousers and either a sweat or a polo shirt top all in the prison colour blue with a S.P.S. badge on the left hand side.

All around the visiting room prison officers either stood on the outskirts or walked among the visitors. There were four prison officers standing in the outskirts of the room and another two walking among the visitors.

As the supervising officer on duty at that time Bruce was positioned in the outskirts of the room.

The prison officer leading Calum and Sarah to the visiting area gestured for them to approach the appropriate visiting table.

Calum and Sarah had not met Sned up until this point so they didn't know what he looked like but Calum did notice a guy in his mid-twenties sitting at an empty table. It had to be Sned.

Calum and Sarah approached the table to see that the guy was in his mid-twenties and looked dishevelled and was probably a junkie.

"Mark Sneddon?" asked Calum as he pulled out a chair from underneath the table and sat down on it directly across from Sned.

"Aye. Who are you?" Sned asked back.

"We're journalists. We work for the Daily Post". said Sarah as she also sat down on a chair opposite Sned.

"Journalists? What the fuck do you want with me?" asked Sned.

"We believe you might know something about a series of murders that have taken place over the last couple of months. Your cousin told us we should come and speak to you." said Calum.

"My cousin? Tony?" said Sned.

"Aye. Tony." started Calum.

"We met him at your gang's HQ, he was with Razzy and a couple of other schemies. We didn't get their names. Tony said to tell you that you should speak to us. It's in your best interests." Calum continued.

"So you're a friend of Razzy's?" asked Sned.

"I wouldn't say we were friends." said Sarah.

"But we definitely know each other." said Calum.

"What do you want to know?" asked Sned.

"We want to know about that old woman up in Aprilfield Drive in Craiglen that you and your mates terrorised to death last year." stated Calum.

"Oh that," replied Sned.

"I don't know if I want to talk about that." Sned continued. There was a brief pause as everyone thought about what they were going to say next.

"Is Tam McGurk still in here?" Calum asked Sned.
Sned paused for a second before answering.
"Aye he is. He's doing life." said Sned.
"So you know him?" asked Calum.
"I know who he is," started Sned.
"He's the incredible hulk. He's probably the scariest guy in here." Sned continued.
"Aye. He is a scary guy." said Calum.
"How do you know him?" asked Sned.
"I know him well. He used to work for my Dad. He's a family friend." explained Calum.
There was a short pause before Calum spoke again.
"Now you can become his new best bud or his new bitch depending on whether or not you tell me what I want to know." said Calum.
There was another short pause before Sned spoke.

"You need to understand that there is a pecking order in here with child killers and sex offenders at the very bottom of the pile but they get segregated away in a wing of their own so the granny bashers are at the bottom of the totem pole in general population." said Sned.
"I don't give a fuck about your place in the pecking order in here." spat out Calum.
"What is it that you want to know?" asked Sned nervously.
"To start with I want the name of everybody that was involved in terrorising Mary Macrae last year. And give me their real names not just their nicknames." said Calum.
There was another short pause before Sned spoke again.
"Well it started off with Bob Campbell." said Sned counting the names with his fingers as he spoke.
"Dead." commented Sarah.
Sned made eye contact with Sarah for the first time before continuing.

"And there was Mark Adam. We called him Sparky." said Sned.

"Also dead." said Sarah.

"And Derek Swanson known as Swanny." said Sned.

"Dead as well." said Sarah.

"And there was David Smith known to us as Smitty."

"Dead." said Sarah.

Sned paused for a few seconds before continuing.

"And Andy McLeod. We call him Cloud." said Sned.

Calum and Sarah looked at each other silently.

"Tell me about this Andy McLeod." said Calum.

"Andy McLeod grew up in the same street I did but and was a year below me going through school so he'll be 23 now." said Sned.

This was an important development for Calum and Sarah. Someone on Brian's hit list that was still alive.

"And he definitely was part of the group that terrorised Mary Macrae?" asked Calum.

"Aye. He was. He didn't go up every time. Maybe just three or four times in total. But he definitely went up a few times." said Sned.

"And how do we contact this Cloud?" asked Sarah.

"If you know Razzy like you say you do Razzy will introduce you to him." said Sned.

There was an uncomfortable pause as Calum and Sarah silently thought about what they were going to do with this new information.

Do they go to the cops?

Do they contact Cloud and let him know his life is in danger?

"I want you to know I didn't want that old Macrae woman to die. None of us did. We just wanted to scare her into dropping the charges against Bob Campbell." said Sned.

"But the tough old bird refused to be bullied and she refused to back down." said Calum.
"Aye. Something like that." said Sned back.
"What did you do?" asked Calum.
"What do you mean what did I do? I just told you everything I know." replied Sned.
"I want to know exactly what you did. Answer me with yes or no." said Calum coldly.
Sned didn't reply at first.
"Did you smash her house windows?" asked Calum.
"Yes." said Sned.
"Did you light fireworks and put them through her letterbox?" asked Calum a little louder than before as he was getting angry.
"Yes." said Sned also a little louder than before.

"Did you kick her door in and hold a knife to her throat?" asked Calum again a little louder than his last question.
At first there was no answer from Sned.
"I said did you kick her door in and hold a knife to her throat?" said Calum almost shouting.
"Yes." said Sned also almost shouting.
Calum stood up angrily.
"You piece of shit." he spat out.
One of the prison officers, Ian, had been walking around the visiting area stepped in and stood in between Calum and Sned.
"Is there a problem here Sneddon?" asked Ian.
Sned exhaled deeply before answering.
"No boss. There's no problem here." he said to Ian.
"What about you?" Ian asked Calum.
"Do you have a problem?" he continued.
"No. No I don't." replied Calum.
"So sit down and finish your visit quietly." said the officer.

Calum slowly sat down at the table across from Sned. Sned leaned into the middle of the table to speak quietly to Calum.
"I'm not exactly proud of what I did but I've got a habit to feed and Campbell said he'd see me alright if I could get her to drop the charges." Sned said to Calum.
Calum didn't speak for a few seconds before replying.
"What's on your tongue?" he asked Sned.
"What?" asked Sned.
"What?" asked Sarah.
"Your tongue. There's something on your tongue." Calum said to Sned.
Calum got out his chair and stepped over to Sned's side of the table and stood next to where Sned was sitting.
"Stand up." Calum said to Sned.

Sned stood up so he was nearly face to face with Calum.
"Now open your mouth and stick your tongue out as far as it will go." said Calum.
Sned opened his mouth and stuck out his tongue as far as it would go.
Calum stared into Sned's mouth.
"Now curl your tongue down onto your chin." said Calum.
Sned complied and curled his tongue down onto his chin.
"How's that?" asked Sned.
"Perfect." said Calum.
Calum took a small step back then hit Sned a powerful uppercut slap hitting him on the point of his chin clamping his mouth shut and severing his tongue in between his teeth.
Sarah screamed out in fright.
Sned instinctively held his hands up to his mouth as the blood started to trickle between his fingers. He wretched a couple of times almost vomiting because of all the blood in

his mouth.

Sned staggered slightly to the left and coughed out a mouthful of blood over a young woman sitting at the table next to his.

The young woman rubbed her hand over her face then looked at her hand to see that Sned had coughed up blood all over her.

The young woman at the table next to where they were standing started to scream.

Sarah got hold of Calum and pulled him away from Sned.

"That's enough." Sarah said to Calum.

"That's not even close to being enough." Calum said to Sarah.

"That's about one percent of what you deserve you junkie piece of shit." Calum spat out at Sned.

By this point Ian the prison officer that had just separated Calum and Sned had rushed over to the scene and had positioned himself between Calum and Sned.

"Stay back." he ordered Calum with his arms outstretched and his metal baton extended.

In just a few seconds Bruce arrived on the scene and also stood between Calum and Sned.

"Take Sneddon to the medical wing and I'll deal with this guy." Bruce said to Ian.

By now a third prison officer had joined the scene and he and Ian had taken Sned by the forearm each to lead him away to the medical wing to see if they could stitch him back up there or to see if they would need to go to the hospital.

By this time Sned was staggering slightly as he was being walked away as he was possibly going into shock. The bottom half of his face and all down the front of his sweatshirt was soaked in blood.

"Time for you to leave." Bruce said to Calum while pointing to the door that lead back to the reception area. Less than a minute later Calum, Sarah and Bruce were at the visitor's lockers. Calum and Sarah were quickly taking their possessions out of the lockers.
Bruce stood beside Calum and he looked over both shoulders before he spoke.
"What the fuck Calum?" he asked.
"I do you a favour and get you a visitor's appointment without making you wait like everybody else and this is how you repay me?" Bruce continued.
"I'm really sorry Bruce. The last thing in the World I wanted was to is to bring grief into your life." replied Calum.
"Sorry isn't good enough Cal. This is my career you are fucking with. There will be a serious incident investigation about this and people are going to ask why you were given a visit so quickly without having to wait like everybody else and I don't know what to tell them." said Bruce.
"Tell them the truth," said Calum.
"Tell them you did an old friend a favour and that same old friend got into a violent confrontation with one of the prisoners and blood was spilled. There is no way you could've known what was going to happen during the visit you arranged." Calum continued.
"That'll have to do." said Bruce.
Sarah had gathered up her belongings and was standing next to Calum waiting for him to finish gathering up his stuff from his locker.
Calum put the last of his belongings into his pocket and was ready to leave.
"Like I said Bruce I'm really sorry." Calum said again.
Bruce exhaled deeply before replying.

"I've been in this job for ten years now without the slightest blemish on my employment record so they probably won't fire me. I'll probably get some kind of official warning and that'll be about it." said Bruce.
"I hope so mate." said Calum as he reached out to shake Bruce's hand.
Bruce paused for a second before shaking Calum's hand.
"Do one thing for me." said Bruce.
"Anything." replied Calum.
"Don't ever ask me to arrange another visit for you. Ever." said Bruce.
"OK." said Calum nodding his head.
Calum and Sarah quickly exited the main building and started walking towards the visitor's car park.

"What was that all about in there?" asked Sarah walking alongside Calum.
"I let that junkie scumbag get under my skin and I shouldn't have." replied Calum.
"So what do we do now?" asked Sarah.
"Now we go home and chill. I'll take you to the police station tomorrow and we'll see what you can find on this Andy Macleod character." said Calum.

Thursday. 9.00pm. West Glasgow.

Calum was in the gym room of his house for his workout. He was dressed the same way he always was for a workout in a pair of tracksuit bottoms and a loose fitting plain white T-shirt.

It was a Thursday night so he would start off with a 12km cycle on the exercise bike.

He started off slowly at first, sitting upright with his hands at his side for the first 2km before leaning forward, speeding up and holding onto the steering grips for the rest.

As his heart rate climbed his mind also began to race.

What was he going to do with this new information about Cloud?

Was he going to warn Cloud?

Was he going to inform the police?

Did he even want the police to know any of what he and Sarah had discovered?

These questions plagued Calum all the way through his workout.

chapter six

Friday. 8.55am. South Glasgow

Calum was parked beside the bus stop across from Sarah's flat waiting to meet up with Sarah. His fingers tapped on the steering wheel and the car's windscreen wipers swiped intermittently to clear the windscreen of the rainwater as it was raining slightly outside.
Calum looked at his watch. It was exactly 8.55am.
Calum noticed Sarah approaching his car from the other side of the road holding up her little black umbrella as she crossed the road.
Sarah opened the passenger door of Calum's car and got in.
"Good morning." she said to Calum as she sat down in the passenger seat.
"Morning," replied Calum as he put the car in gear and drove off.
"So you know what you'll be looking for. Anything you can find on Andy McLeod. Criminal record. Driving license. Social media." said Calum.
"Yes," replied Sarah.
"This won't take long. Maybe two hours max." Sarah continued.
"Good," said Calum.
"Maybe we can contact this little bastard before Brian catches up with him." Calum continued.
There was a brief pause before Sarah spoke up.
"Do you know what you want to do moving forward?" she asked Calum.

"What do you mean?" replied Calum.
"What do you want to do with this new information we have about Sned and Cloud?
Do we take it to the police?
Do we warn Cloud his life is in danger?
Do we just run the story and let the chips fall where they may?" Sarah asked.
"I don't know," said Calum.
"I haven't decided yet." he continued.
"I want you to know that whatever you decide to do I'm with you." said Sarah.
"That's good to know." replied Calum.
Calum didn't really speak the rest of the way to Maryhill police station as he was deep in thought. In fact he didn't speak at all until he drove his car into the car park at the front of the building.
"OK here we are." said Calum as he stopped his car outside the main entrance.
Sarah started to unfasten her seatbelt.
"I've got something I need to do but you can call me as soon as you've found what you need about Cloud." said Calum.
"Will do." replied Sarah.
Sarah got out the car and made her way to the entrance of the building quickly walking though the main entrance doors into the reception corridor and she flashed her ID badge at the police officer as she made her way to the doorway at the far end of the corridor.
The police officer at the reception window nodded her head in acknowledgement as Sarah passed by.
Sarah reached the doorway at the end of the corridor and swiped her badge on the scanner to open the door.

The green light on the scanner lit up, the door opened and Sarah walked through.

Friday. 9.35am. Central Glasgow

Calum was walking away from his parked car at Sighthill cemetery in Central Glasgow. It was raining slightly and he was dressed as he nearly always was in a smart suit with a white shirt and no tie. He was also carrying a bottle of Jameson whisky in a brown paper bag.
He made his way along the long curving footpath in the cemetery that lead to his father's grave in the North Western corner of the graveyard.
After a few minutes Calum arrived at his destination, a large granite Celtic cross headstone with the family name McCulkin engraved into the centre of it.
Calum stood on the grass in front of the headstone for a few seconds looking at the unkempt state of the burial plot. There were weeds growing next to the gravestone and dead leaves of flowers from other plots had blown across the cemetery and came to rest on the patch of grass in front of the McCulkin headstone.
Calum took the bottle out of the bag, placed the bottle on the ledge of the bottom of the headstone and started to pull out the weeds at the plot.
"Hello Dad." Calum said as he pulled out the weeds with his bare hands and put the weeds into the paper bag the whisky was in.
"I know it's been a while since I was last here. Too long actually. Far too long. I thought I'd come and see you because I need some advice. Your advice." Calum continued as he finished off the weeding and moved onto picking up the dead leaves that had blown onto the plot from other graves.
"The situation is that I've been investigating a group of murders that have happened over the last couple of months and I have found the guy that has been committing them

and I don't know what to do" said Calum picking up the leaves and putting them into the paper bag as he talked.
"If I step in and go to the authorities with what I have a good man will go to jail probably for the rest of his life and a couple of scumbags will get away with committing a despicable crime. If I do nothing at least one and possibly two scumbags will get killed.
I know it sounds straightforward enough and I should just let the scumbags die but I've been thinking about the impact the murders would have on their families because the two scumbags I'm talking about are just young guys. Both of them are still in their twenties and they are both somebody's brother and somebody's son and their murders would devastate their families." said Calum as he picked up the last of the leaves and put them into the paper bag he was holding.
"I've got a work colleague looking into getting an address for one of these scumbags and I don't know what I'm going to do with the information. Do I warn him? Do I go to the cops? Do I do nothing and just let the situation play out? You used to always say that very few situations are as straightforward as simply being right or wrong. You used to say that many situations you might find yourself in life exist in varying shades of grey not just black or white". Calum placed his left hand on the headstone.
"I need to know what you would do." Calum said softly.
Calum paused for a few seconds before picking up the bottle of whisky.
"I've brought you a bottle of your favourite whisky, Jameson."
Calum slowly unscrewed the lid and opened up the bottle. Calum took a few steps back and slowly started to pour the whisky onto the grassed area in front of the headstone.

"I know that if you're up there watching you'll send me a sign." said Calum as he poured the last of the whisky onto the grass.

Calum slowly screwed the lid back onto the whisky bottle and glanced to his right to four plots up where he saw a magpie on the grass.

Calum turned around to face the bird and to watch what it was doing.

The magpie was hopping around on the grass trying to pick something up. Probably a worm or a large insect.

After four or five unsuccessful attempts to pick the object up the magpie flew up and sat on top of the gravestone all the time watching the patch of grass it had just been on.

After a few seconds the magpie hopped of the gravestone onto the patch of grass and quickly picked up a large worm and then flew away.

Calum smiled and put his left hand on his father's gravestone.

"Got it Dad. Got it." he said quietly before walking away towards his parked car.

Friday. 11.20am. North West Glasgow

Calum was sitting in his car parked outside Maryhill police station waiting for Sarah to exit the building. It was raining lightly outside and he was tapping his fingers on the steering wheel in time with the windscreen wipers on the front window of his car.
After several minutes Sarah appeared at the main doorway to the building holding her small black umbrella in one hand and a blue cardboard folder in the other.
Sarah quickly made her way out of the police station and into Calum's waiting car.
"Hello again." she said as she sat down on the passenger seat.
"How did you get on? Any joy?" asked Calum as he started to drive away back to his place to look over whatever Sarah had found.
"Yes. I found a few bits and pieces." replied Sarah.
"That's good." said Calum.
After a few minutes driving Calum spoke up.
"I've made a decision about how I want to proceed," said Calum.
"I've had an epiphany." said Calum.
"An epiphany?" asked Sarah.
"It means a moment of clarity." said Calum.
"I know what an epiphany is. I'm just curious about yours." said Sarah.
"Well I had been wondering what to do next with the information we've uncovered and I couldn't help but wonder what my dad would've done." said Calum.
"And?" asked Sarah.
"My Dad believed in second chances and I think my Dad would've given this Cloud character a second chance." stated Calum.

"Really?" asked Sarah.

"Not a pass for the crimes he's committed and been part of. He needs to own up and face justice for what he's done. But if he does we'll do whatever we can to save his life from Brian." said Calum.

"Do you really think this guy is going to stick his hand up and confess to a serious crime that will get him jailed?" asked Sarah.

"No. No I don't. But I want to give him the choice." said Calum.

"So what happens when this guy refuses our offer?" asked Sarah.

"Then fuck him." said Calum coldly.

Friday. 12.00pm. West Glasgow

Calum and Sarah had just entered Calum's kitchen area, a large and fully equipped open-plan futuristic white marble effect area centred around a huge aluminium affect American style fridge freezer with a large white marble effect island in the middle of the room.
Calum opened the fridge door as Sarah placed her blue cardboard folder down onto the kitchen island.
"Do you want a drink?" asked Calum.
"I'll take a mineral water if you've got one." Sarah replied.
Calum picked up 2 bottles of mineral water from the fridge and stepped over to the kitchen island to hand a bottle of water to Sarah.
Sarah unscrewed the lid from the bottle of water and took a swig.
"So tell me about Cloud." said Calum as he took a swig from his water bottle.
Sarah placed her water bottle down on the island then opened up the blue folder and started looking through the printed off documents in the folder.
"OK then," she started.
"Andrew McLeod known as Cloud. Age 23 years. Previous convictions for assault and aggravated assault. Had managed to avoid prison until around 2 years ago when he got 18 months for possession of an offensive weapon. A knife. He served 9 months and was out of prison on license around the time Mary Macrae was being terrorised." Sarah continued.
"That probably explains why he only went along with the others a few times instead of every time. He didn't want to get picked up by the cops because he'd get sent straight back to jail." said Calum.
"Possibly." said Sarah.

"Do you have a picture of him?" asked Calum.
"Yes. Yes I do." said Sarah as she quickly rifled through the paperwork in front of her.
"Here you are." said Sarah as she handed Calum a piece of paper with a police mugshot of Cloud on it.
Calum studied the picture of Cloud.
"He even looks like a little rat." Calum said quietly.
Sarah looked through the paperwork in front of her until she found what she was looking for.
"I've got a last known address for him. It's his mum's place in Burns Street in Craiglen." said Sarah as she handed Calum the relevant piece of paper.
"What do you think?" asked Sarah.
"I think it's time we paid this son of a bitch Cloud a visit." said Calum.

Friday. 1.25pm. North Glasgow

Calum was driving his car slowly along Burns Street in Craiglen looking for number 39, Cloud's mum's home and his last known address. Sarah sat in the passenger seat in Calum's car counting the house doors as they passed by. The houses in Burns Street were all the same, square concrete buildings with a small flat area out the front of each one where most residents had put up clothes washing lines while others used it as storage for children's prams and partly disassembled mountain bikes and motorbikes. There was little to no greenery in Burns Street, just bricks and concrete everywhere with odd numbered houses on the left and even numbers on the right.
Sarah counted the numbers out loud as they passed.
"27, 29, 31, 33, 35, 37, 39. That's us right there. Number 39. The one with the red door." she said while pointing at door number 39.
Calum pulled the car over to the side of the road and stopped.
"How do you want to play this?" asked Sarah knowing full well that the last two interviews Calum had performed had ended in violence.
"What do you think?" asked Calum.
Sarah paused for a second before answering.
"I think we should play it straight down the line. No threats and no bullying. We try to convince him that he should own up to what he has done and if he does we could help him." said Sarah.
"And if he doesn't?" asked Calum.
"Then like you said. Fuck him." replied Sarah.
"Sounds like a plan." said Calum smiling as he got out the car.
Sarah also got out the car and walked alongside Calum

along the path leading up to the front door of number 39 Burns Street, Craiglen.

"Here we go." said Calum as he pressed the doorbell.

After a few seconds Cloud's mum, Sharon, answered the door. She was probably in her mid to late forties and was dressed in a tracksuit and trainers just like the schemies Calum and Sarah had met at the CYT headquarters the other day.

There was a good chance that Cloud's mum Sharon was also a schemie making Cloud a second generation schemie. Possibly more.

Sharon took the home made roll-up cigarette out of her mouth before speaking.

"What do you want?" she asked.

"We'd like to speak to Andy McLeod known as Cloud." said Calum.

"Are you the police?" asked Sharon.

"No. We're journalists." offered Sarah.

"Journalists? What the fuck do you want with my Andrew?" asked Sharon.

"We'd like to speak to him about a true crime piece we're working on." said Calum.

Sharon inhaled deeply on the roll-up cigarette in her hand and blew the smoke towards Calum's face.

"Andrew," she shouted back into the house.

"There's a couple of journalists at the door wanting to talk to you." she continued.

A few seconds later Cloud arrived at the front door to speak to Calum and Sarah.

He was dressed the same way he always was wearing a blue and white tracksuit, trainers and a skip cap and he was quite pasty faced, pale, and he looked like he could do with seeing some sunlight just like the rest of the CYT they had met so far.

"What do you want?" Cloud asked when he reached the doorway.

"We want to speak to you about some criminality you were involved in last year." said Calum.

"Really?" said Cloud.

"What criminality is that?" he continued.

"The terrorising to death of a defenceless senior citizen. Mary Macrae." Calum said coldly.

Cloud paused for a second before answering.

"I heard she died of natural causes. A heart attack." said Cloud.

"That might be the cause of death named on the death certificate but we both know that she was terrorised to death by you and your schemie mates trying to get her to drop the charges against Bobby Campbell." said Calum.

Again Cloud paused before answering.

"You might be right. So what do you want me to do about it?" Cloud asked.

"We would like you to put your hand up and take responsibility for what you've done." said Calum.

"And how would I do that?" Cloud asked.

"You could go to your nearest police station and confess." said Calum.

Cloud found this idea funny.

"So you want me to go to the nearest cop shop and confess to a crime the police aren't even investigating?" he said to Calum almost laughing he spoke.

"That's right." said Calum.

"You must think that I'm a complete idiot. A pure dafty." said Cloud.

"Almost everyone that was involved is dead now. It's just you and Sned left. So you wouldn't be snitching on anyone." said Sarah.

"And why the fuck would I do what you're suggesting?" asked Cloud.

Calum and Sarah looked at each other before Calum gestured with his hand for Sarah to answer him.

"Because your life is in real danger." said Sarah.

"Really?" said Cloud sarcastically.

"You must have noticed that the four of your mates that have been murdered in the last 2 months are the same mates that terrorised Mary Macrae?" said Sarah.

"I never really thought about it much. We were involved in a lot of stuff together over the years." said Cloud.

"Well you should think about it a lot." offered Calum.

"If you confess to the cops we'll work with them to try and keep you safe." said Sarah.

"And how would you do that?" asked Cloud.

Calum and Sarah looked at each other again before Calum answered.

"We've got a pretty good idea who it is that's after you. We could let the cops know." offered Calum.

"And who is it that's after me?" asked Cloud.

"We're not at liberty to say." said Calum.

Cloud smiled. He thought he had worked out what was really going on.

"I think you two are trying to play me," he said.

"I think you're trying to create a story to print in your paper. I think telling me my life is in danger is bullshit." he spat out.

"It's not bullshit Cloud. You've got 4 dead mates that prove somebody is targeting CYT members and the guys that terrorised Mary Macrae in particular." said Calum.

"No. I'm not falling for it." said Cloud.

"This is the only chance that you're going to get." said

Calum.

Calum reached into his jacket inside pocket and took out one of his business cards and handed it to Cloud.

"My phone number and email address are both listed on this card. Get in touch if or when you change your mind." said Calum coldly.

Cloud looked at the card in his hand then quickly tore it in half and threw it back into Calum's face.

"Go and fuck yourself. Both of you." Cloud spat out.

Calum paused for a second before responding. Part of him wanted to beat the shit out of Cloud but on this occasion he managed to control his primal urge.

"OK. You've been warned. If you choose to ignore the warning, then that's up to you." said Calum calmly.

"Let's go." he said to Sarah as he started to walk back to the car. Sarah followed behind him.

Less than a minute later Calum and Sarah were sitting in Calum's car ready to leave Craiglen.

"I thought you were going to smash him back there when he tore up your business card and threw it in your face." said Sarah.

"Part of me wanted to but I must be getting calmer in my old age." said Calum as he started the car up.

"So what do we do now?" asked Sarah.

"I don't know," said Calum.

"But I do know that I don't want to see Brian jailed for taking out these wee scumbags." he continued.

"So what can we do?" asked Sarah.

"I don't know. Give me the weekend to think about it. I should have a plan by Monday morning." said Calum.

"OK." said Sarah.

Calum looked at his watch. It was almost 1.45pm.

"Are you hungry?" he asked Sarah.

"I could eat something." she replied.
"I know the very place." said Calum.

Friday. 2.10pm. West Glasgow.

Calum and Sarah were sitting down at opposite sides of a large circular dining table in Calum's Italian themed restaurant Francesco's in Glasgow's trendy West End. The restaurant consisted of 14 large circular tables each approximately 5 feet in diameter and big enough to comfortably sit 6 people at each table.
Each table was covered in white silk table cloth and all around the restaurant there were life-sized replica marble statues of various Roman and Greek deities.
Large but tasteful chandeliers hung from the ceiling and there was a bar area at the rear of the restaurant with waist high bar stools along the side of it.
The entire restaurant was busy with all of the dining tables filled to capacity and all of the bar stools were in use with people waiting for a table to become available.
Several suited waiters skilfully walked and weaved between the tables bringing food and drinks and bills to the customers.
"This place is really nice Calum. I'm impressed you managed to get us a table at such short notice." said Sarah adjusting her sitting position and looking through the drinks menu.
"Well I suppose it helps if you own the place." said Calum.
"This is your place?" asked Sarah almost in disbelief.
"This is the restaurant your Dad left you?" she continued as she leaned across the table.
Calum paused for a second before answering.
"Aye it is." he said.
One of the waiters, Nino, approached the table.
"Good afternoon Mr. McCulkin." said Nino in his half Italian and half Glaswegian accent that he had developed after growing up in Italy but spending the last 20 years

waiting on tables in Glasgow.

"Would you like to order any drinks?" Nino continued.

"I'll have a bottle of mineral water." said Calum as Nino took notes on his little notepad he was carrying.

"And the good lady?" said Nino turning to face Sarah.

"I'll have a large glass of Prosecco please." said Sarah.

"Excellent choice," said Nino as he quickly jotted down the information.

"I will return in 2 minutes." he said as he quickly walked away to collect the order.

Sarah leaned across the table to speak quietly to Calum.

"Around the city. How many other upmarket restaurants do you think are really a front for organised crime?" she asked quietly.

Calum leaned towards Sarah to answer her quietly.

"This place is not a front. It never has been. It was set up with clean money and has only ever processed clean money," said Calum leaning back into his seat.

"As for what other groups get up to who knows? There will definitely be a few maybe more than just a few. Your guess is as good as mine." Calum continued.

Sarah also leaned back into her seat nodding her head in agreement.

Nino arrived with the drinks on a silver tray. He handed Sarah her wine first.

"For the lady." he said as he placed Sarah's wine glass down on the table in front of her.

"Thanks." said Sarah.

"And for Mr. McCulkin" Nino said as placed a glass bottle of upmarket mineral water and a glass down on the table in front of Calum.

"Thanks Nino." said Calum.

"And also for the lady." said Nino as he took a menu off his tray and handed it to Sarah.

"Thank you." said Sarah.

"And also for Mr. McCulkin." said Nino as he handed Calum a copy of the menu from his tray.

"Thanks again." replied Calum.

"I wait for you at bar. When you ready to order. You signal me. I come straight away." said Nino before walking away to stand at the bar to await Calum's signal.

Sarah took a small sip of her wine and opened up the menu.

"So what would you recommend Mr. McCulkin?" asked Sarah playfully mimicking Nino's Glaswegian Italian accent.

Calum smiled as he answered.

"The ham and mushroom tagliatelle is really good. Maybe the best in the city. The spaghetti carbonara is also really good. I'm going to go with the tagliatelle." said Calum.

Sarah quickly scanned through the menu.

"I think I'll try the carbonara." said Sarah.

"Good choice." said Calum.

"Are you ready to order?" he continued.

"Yes." said Sarah.

"OK" said Calum as he looked over at Nino standing at the bar and he raised his hand to head height to get Nino's attention.

Nino instantly noticed Calum's hand signal and quickly made his way over to the table.

"You are ready to order Mr. McCulkin?" asked Nino.

Calum gestured across the table towards Sarah.

"Ladies first I think Nino." said Calum.

"Of course Mr. McCulkin." replied Nino as he stepped over towards Sarah his notepad and pen in hand.

"What would the good lady like?" asked Nino.

"I would like the spaghetti carbonara please." said Sarah.
"Excellent choice Bella donna," said Nino as he quickly jotted down the order.
"And for Mr. McCulkin?" he asked as he turned around to face Calum.
"I'll have my usual please Nino. The ham and mushroom tagliatelle." said Calum.
"Also an excellent choice," said Nino as he wrote on his notepad.
"Anything else?" inquired Nino.
"A side order. Chips? Bread sticks? Garlic bread?" he continued.
"No Nino I think we're good." said Calum as he poured some of his mineral water into the glass it came with.
"OK I go now but I return soon with your food." said Nino before walking away from the table towards the kitchen area of the restaurant.
Sarah leaned across the table to speak quietly to Calum.
"Now that's what I call effective customer service." she said quietly to Calum.
"Like I said. It helps if you own the place." said Calum as he took a drink from his glass of water.
15 minutes later Calum and Sarah were eating their meal. Sarah stopped eating for a few seconds then took a drink from her wine glass.
"So how do you see this situation with Brian playing out?" she asked Calum fully aware that they were in a fairly crowded public place and someone may overhear their conversation so she shouldn't mention killings or murder.
Calum took a sip from his water before answering.
"I don't know. I really don't know." was his reply.
"We need to formulate a plan soon Calum. Our boss, Bobby, will probably be wanting a progress report from us

soon," said Sarah.

"Not to mention the cops. They'll probably be looking through the files I've been accessing on their system. It's just a matter of time before they put the pieces together the same way we did." Sarah continued.

Calum paused for a few seconds before replying.

This was something he hadn't thought of.

What if the cops were just pretending to give Sarah and him carte blanche access to their computer system?

What if every search Sarah performed and every file she printed off was being logged somewhere to be examined later?

Calum couldn't be absolutely sure that was what was going on but it was highly likely that it was.

"Give me the weekend to think about it." said Calum calmly.

"OK," said Sarah.

"But take this into consideration. Any cover story we create to divert attention away from Brian will need to include details that would explain all of the events so far and for events that haven't happened yet. Do you know what I'm talking about?" said Sarah.

"Yes" said Calum. He knew exactly what Sarah was talking about.

chapter seven

Saturday. 3.18am. West Glasgow

Calum was deep asleep in his bed at his home in the West of Glasgow. The room was in total darkness apart from the digital display on his bedside alarm clock that read 03:18 in glowing red light.
Out of the darkness stepped Brian dressed in black with black shoes, black trousers, black polo neck jersey and a black ski-mask with holes only for his eyes and mouth. In his right hand he held a Glock 17 pistol.
Brian leaned over the sleeping Calum for a few seconds before making his move.
Brian placed his left hand over Calum's mouth and tapped Calum on the head with the pistol in his right hand.
"Wake up Calum." he said to Calum.
Calum woke up quickly, startled at first.
"What the?" said Calum through Brian's hand.
"Shhh. Take it easy McCulkin." said Brian as he held the business end of the Glock to Calum's head.
"Get up." ordered Brian.
Calum quickly got out of bed wearing his tartan pyjama bottoms and a baggy white T-shirt. He held his hands up at head height.
"What do you want?" he asked Brian.
"I want to have a friendly little chat." said Brian.
"Now move. We're going through to your living room." said Brian now standing behind Calum with the pistol still pointed at Calum's head.

Calum started to slowly walk out of the bedroom and down the stairs to his living room.

After about a minute or so the pair had reached Calum's living room, a modern man-cave style room with a 3-seater black leather couch on the right as you enter the room and another on the left, 2 single chairs at the far left and a giant 72 inch plasma TV mounted on the wall in the centre of the room.

Brian switched on the light and pushed Calum onto the sofa on the right.

"Sit down." he said as he closed the door and made his way towards one of the single chairs at the far left of the room. Brian sat down on one of the single seaters and placed his Glock on the chair's right hand side arm rests with his hand sitting on top of the gun.

"Do you know who I am?" Brian asked.

"Yes" said Calum.

"Who am I?" asked Brian.

"You are Brian Macrae. Grandson of Mary Macrae. Formerly of Aprilfield Drive Craiglen now living in Hereford where you are based with the S.A.S. You probably called in a favour from someone you know in military intelligence or M.I.5 to get a billing address for the mobile phone number on the business card I gave your neighbour" said Calum calmly.

"Very good. Now do you know why I'm here?" asked Brian.

"You're here to scare me off the story I've been investigating. The story of the CYT scumbags that have been getting killed over the last 2 months," said Calum.

"I know that you are the one that has been killing them. You change your method with each kill to try and throw the cops off the scent but the fact that every kill was committed by someone that knows exactly what they are doing links them all together." Calum continued.

"And?" asked Brian.

"And I don't believe you are here to do me any real harm." said Calum.

"And why is that?" asked Brian.

"If you wanted to kill me you wouldn't have woke me up. You would have just killed me in my sleep. And if you were going to use that Glock you would have brought a silencer," started Calum.

"You're just here to give me a good scare. You're a killer but not a murderer." Calum continued.

"You see a lot." said Brian.

"I know what those CYT bastards did to your Gran and I'm on your side Brian. We both are. Me and my work colleague who has been investigating the killings with me. Neither one of us wants to see you jailed over what you've been doing," said Calum.

"We have the power to point the authorities in the wrong direction. To get them chasing ghosts." Calum continued.

"And why would you do that?" asked Brian.

"Because I believe in justice Brian. And my family name is McCulkin. Donald McCulkin was my father. If you don't know who he was you can just Google him. Donald McCulkin Glasgow. You'll see that my family are not friends of the police. Far from it." said Calum.

"I know who your Dad was." said Brian.

"Then you'll know that I mean what I say when I say I can be an ally to you. I can help you." said Calum.

"Help me how?" inquired Brian.

"I know that you've got 2 more guys on your kill list. Mark Sneddon and Andy Mcleod. Sned and Cloud. I'm sure you know that Sned is in the clink right now so you can't get at

him but I know people that are in there with him. Dangerous people. The kind of people that would kill him just for being a granny basher with no need for money to change hands." said Calum.
Brian paused before replying.
"What else can you do to help me?" he asked.

"Well I can set you up with a disposable stolen car for a start," said Calum.
"And I can help you dispose of a body. I can get you access to a wood chipper or a blast furnace or a scrapyard car compacter with no questions asked." Calum continued.
"And what makes you think I need your help?" asked Brian.
"The more bodies you drop around Glasgow the more police officers will be assigned to investigate the murders and sooner or later someone will put the pieces together just like I did. You need to start disposing of bodies and that's a 2-man job." stated Calum.
Again Brian paused before replying.
"Why should I believe anything you say? Why should I trust you not to call the cops as soon as I leave?" asked Brian.
"Because I'm a McCulkin. The son of Donald McCulkin. I'm a man of my word and I don't snitch. Ever." said Calum.
Yet again Brian paused for a few seconds to process what was being said then pulled up the front of his ski mask so Calum could see his face.
"Well it looks like I've now got a partner." said Brian.
"If you want my help." said Calum back.
"OK but understand this. If you try to set me up or I get the feeling you are trying to set me up I will kill you. No hesitation and no second chances." said Brian coldly.

"That's fair enough." said Calum.
Brian stood up to exit the room.
Calum also stood up.
"I'll show you out." said Calum.
"Don't bother," said Brian.
"I'll see myself out." Brian continued.

Calum sat back down on the couch and exhaled deeply.

chapter eight

Saturday. 10.10am. South Glasgow.

Calum was sitting in his car parked at the bus stop across from Sarah's flat. He was dressed casually in jeans and a black shirt. His forefingers were tapping on the steering wheel in time with the song being played on the radio. The weather outside was dry but overcast. It was the first time he had been to Sarah's place and it wasn't raining. He looked at his watch on his right wrist and it was 10.10am exactly.

Out of the corner of his eye on his right hand side he noticed Sarah making her way across the road towards his car. She was dressed casually but smartly in baggy trousers and a white silk shirt.

Sarah quickly crossed the road and opened up the passenger side door and got in.

"I wasn't expecting to hear from you until Monday morning. What's up?" she asked.

Calum put the car in gear and started to drive away.

"Brian payed me a visit last night. Well technically this morning" said Calum.

"Brian?" asked Sarah.

"Brian Macrae? The Brian we've been investigating? What the fuck did he want?" Sarah continued.

"He woke me up just after 3 this morning and put a gun to my head," said Calum.

"Then he walked me through to my living room and we had chat." Calum continued.

"A chat? What did you chat about?" asked Sarah.
"We talked about how much I knew about what he was doing and what he was planning to do." said Calum.
"This is getting dangerous Calum." said Sarah.
"I don't think so. I don't think he was ever going to do me any harm. I think he just wanted to scare me off the story." replied Calum.
"And what is the story we're going to go with Calum? Bobby McCiver will be wanting an update from us on Monday. What are we going to tell him?" said Sarah.
"We'll tell him we're close to finishing off our investigations and we'll have the story by the end of the week." said Calum calmly.
"Is there anything else I should know about your conversation with the guy who is basically a serial killer that we've been investigating?" asked Sarah.
Calum paused for a few seconds before answering.
"I agreed to help him get the last 2 guys on his hit list. Sned and Cloud." said Calum knowing Sarah would not be happy about the arrangement.
"You did what?" she said loudly almost shouting.
"Have you completely lost your fucking mind?" she continued loudly.
This is why Calum wanted to speak to her in his car and not in her house where her roommate would overhear raised voices or at least one raised voice. Sarah's.
"If you get caught and convicted for 2 counts of conspiracy to commit murder you could get 20 years," she said sternly.
"And that's assuming he doesn't just kill you when you've outlived your usefulness. Have you even thought about that? You do remember what your mate Donny told us at the paintball place we visited don't you? Killing for this guy is as easy as blowing out a candle and you shouldn't

fuck with this guy in any way." Sarah continued.
"It won't come to that." said Calum.
"How do you know that?" asked Sarah.
"All you know about this guy is that he is a trained professional killer that has killed 4 guys in quick succession so far over the last couple of months and is planning to kill 2 more soon." Sarah continued.
"The point is that they all deserved it." offered Calum.
"Maybe so. But what if we're wrong about this guy? What if he is not a good guy out for revenge? What if it turns out he is a complete psychopath and he will kill anyone that pisses him off?" said Sarah.

"I don't think that's the case." said Calum.
"And how would you know that? Do you honestly think that you're in a position to accurately say what this guy is and isn't capable of because you spent 5 minutes talking with him after he pulled a gun on you?" said Sarah.
"I just feel it in my gut that this guy isn't a threat to me or anyone else that doesn't deserve it and I'm going to help him." said Calum calmly.
"This is a really fucking bad idea Calum. This guy is not one of your mates. You don't owe him anything." said Sarah.
A few seconds passed before anyone spoke again.
"You said you were with me whatever I decided to do." said Calum.
"That's when we were just planning to create a false narrative for the cops to follow not actually getting involved in the killing of anyone," replied Sarah.
"What kind of help does he want from you anyway?" Sarah continued.
"I told him I could get him a disposable stolen car and that

I could arrange for him to get access to a wood chipper, a blast furnace or a scrapyard car compactor to dispose of a body." said Calum.

"That's it?" asked Sarah.

"And I told him I knew people in prison beside Sned that would happily kill him for being a granny basher," said Calum.

"That's it. He said he'd contact me when he needs me." Calum continued.

"Well at least he hasn't talked you into killing anyone." offered Sarah beginning to calm down.

"No. No. No. Nothing like that. I'll just be supplying him with disposable transport, I'll be introducing him to someone that can help him dispose of a body and I'll be writing a letter to an old family friend in prison and that's it." said Calum.

"OK but if you turn up dead or if you go missing I'm going straight to the cops with everything I've got on Brian and the CYT." said Sarah.

"That's fine. But it won't come to that." said Calum.

"I just hope you know what you are doing because it's your liberty and possibly your life you are gambling with Calum." said Sarah.

"I know what I'm doing. I'll be fine." said Calum.

chapter nine

Monday. 10.00am. Daily Post HQ. Glasgow.

It was 10 am at the Daily Post's HQ in Glasgow on the banks of the river Clyde.
Calum and Sarah were sitting on 2 out of 4 plastic chairs in the lobby outside Bobby McCiver's office.
Calum was dressed in a smart suit with a white shirt but no tie and Sarah was dressed in a smart trouser suit.
It was a busy newspaper production environment and all around them people were rushing around holding folders and paperwork and talking into mobile phones.
"Just let me do the talking when we get in here," said Calum.
"I'll spin him a line and get us another week to finish our story." Calum continued.
"OK. But I'm still not happy about you getting involved with Brian." said Sarah.
"I told you not to worry about it. I've got that situation under control." said Calum.
Bobby poked his head out of his office door and turned to the right to look at Calum and Sarah.
"Come on in guys." he said to them both.
Calum and Sarah immediately got up and walked into Bobby's office.
Nothing in Bobby's office had changed in the last week since they were both in it.
Inside his office there was a large leather swivel chair that Bobby would sit in with his back to the windows, a large

wooden desk with a keyboard and computer monitor sitting on it, a pile of paper folders all packed full of documents and two smaller swivel chairs on the near side of the desk. Bobby sat down on the large leather chair with his back to the window and gestured for Calum and Sarah to sit in the unused swivel chairs on the other side of the desk from him.

"Please. Both of you take a seat." he said to Calum and Sarah.

Calum and Sarah immediately sat down on the chairs.

"So guys, how is the investigation into the CYT killings going?" he asked Calum and Sarah.

Calum cleared his throat before replying.

"We're making slow progress but we're definitely moving forward with our inquiries." said Calum.

"That's good to hear." said Bobby.

"How much longer do you think you will need to complete this story?" asked Bobby.

Calum and Sarah looked at each other before Calum answered.

"I'd say about a week maybe a week and a bit." said Calum.

"OK" said Bobby.

"You're not saying much Sarah. Have the remaining members of the CYT been opening up to you both?" he asked Sarah.

"It's not been easy gaining their trust. But we're definitely moving in the right direction." said Sarah nervously. She wasn't a good liar.

"And I'm curious. What direction is that exactly?" asked Bobby.

"Excuse me?" asked Sarah.

"What has been going on? Why have the gang members

been killed? You don't have to give me the exact details of every murder. I just want to know what it's all been about." said Bobby to Sarah.

"It uh. It. It. It looks like it's an internal dispute within the gang." said Sarah.

"Interesting." said Bobby as he leaned back into his chair.

"The gang has a strict no snitching policy and that's probably why the gang members have been reluctant to talk us." said Calum trying to get back into the conversation because Sarah was finding lying to Bobby stressful.

"I see." said Bobby.

"Like I said if you give us another week and a bit we should have the full story ready for you to run with." offered Calum.

"OK" said Bobby nodding his head.

"I'll give you both another 2 weeks. If you don't have everything with this story wrapped up and ready to print I'll take you both off the story and put you onto something else. There's no point keeping you on this story if nobody who knows anything wants to talk to you." stated Bobby.

"That should do it." said Calum.

"That'll be enough time, I think." said Sarah.

"And if and when you write up the story I want you to email it to me. Any time of the day or night. I want to read it as soon as it is written," said Bobby.

"OK then guys. That'll be all." said Bobby as he stood up to walk Calum and Sarah out of the office.

Calum and Sarah stood up and started walking towards the door.

"Keep up the good work guys. As far as I know there isn't another newspaper in the country that is investigating this story." said Bobby as Calum and Sarah exited his office.

Calum and Sarah started to walk along the hallway from

Bobby's office to the elevator at the far end that lead to the underground carpark where Calum had parked his car. Calum pressed the button for the elevator and looked around to make sure no-one was within earshot to overhear what he was going to say.

"An internal dispute within the gang?" he asked Sarah.

The elevator doors opened and Calum and Sarah got in. Calum pressed the button for the carpark on the lower ground floor and the doors closed again.

"I'm sorry. It was the best I could come up with when Bobby put me on the spot. I'm not a good liar. Never have been." said Sarah.

Calum found the fact that Sarah couldn't lie well as being an endearing part of her personality.

"It's OK," Calum reassured her.

"It's not the worst cover story I've ever heard. We can work with it and make it work for what we need it to." Calum continued.

The elevator doors opened. Calum and Sarah got out and into the underground carpark and started walking towards Calum's parked car.

"We need to sit down and get our story straight," said Calum.

"We can use the story you gave Bobby as a framework and we can make out that the dead guys were all involved in a violent tit for tat struggle within the gang." Calum continued.

"That sounds plausible apart from one thing." offered Sarah.

"And what's that?" asked Calum.

"You'll need at least one guy to still be alive. Somebody has to be alive and guilty of the latest murder." stated Sarah.

"I'll need to work on that." said Calum.

Calum and Sarah reached Calum's car. Calum unlocked the car with the remote key fob and they both got in.

As soon as they both sat down in the car Calum's phone started to ring. Calum put his phone in the phone holder rack in the centre of the dashboard to talk to the caller hands free. The phone was displaying a mobile phone number but no name as Calum didn't have this number stored in his phone. This was not unusual for Calum as he gave his business cards out to quite a few people and some of them would call him up from their own mobiles.

Calum pressed the answer button on his phone.

"Hello?" said Calum.

No answer.

"Hello?" he asked again.

"Calum this is Brian." said Brian's voice on the phone.

Calum instantly held his forefinger up to his mouth signalling Sarah to remain silent. Sarah silently nodded her head in agreement.

"What can I do for you Brian?" asked Calum.

"Were you serious when you said you could help me out with a few things?" asked Brian.

"I was absolutely serious." said Calum.

"Good. I need a car for a day or two. Something reliable that won't attract too much attention and something with a lot of boot space." said Brian.

Calum paused for a few seconds before answering.

"I can arrange that no problem. I know exactly the guy to speak to." said Calum.

"I'll come to your place tonight at 9 o'clock and we can go and pick the car up." said Brian.

"OK" said Calum.

"You can reach me on this number I'm using. I'll be using

it for the next few days. You should store it in your phone." said Brian.

"Cool. I'll speak to you later." said Calum.

Brian ended the conversation.

Neither Calum or Sarah said anything for a few seconds.

"What do you think?" asked Calum.

"I think that you are playing a very dangerous game with a very dangerous man," said Sarah.

"I hope you are reading this guy right when you say he's not a threat to you." she continued.

"Well you know what to do if I turn up dead or go missing." said Calum.

chapter ten

Monday. 9.00pm. West Glasgow

It was 9pm in the West End of Glasgow and Calum was pacing up and down his living room anxiously waiting for Brian to make contact so they could go and pick up a disposable car.
He was still dressed in the same smart suit and white shirt from earlier and he was holding a small bottle of mineral water in his left hand and was taking small swigs from it as he paced back and forth.
He thought about what Sarah had said about Brian possibly being psychotic and that he would maybe just kill him when he had outlived his usefulness.
The truth was that Calum hadn't even thought about that possibility. He had got so strung up in empathising with Brian's need for revenge that he had thought about very little else.
He looked at his watch on his right wrist and it was exactly 9pm.
His mobile phone started ringing.
Calum took his phone out of his trouser pocket and looked at the caller display information. It was Brian.
"Right on time." Calum said quietly to himself.
Calum answered the phone.
"Hello." he said.
"I'm standing in your driveway," said Brian on the other

end of the call.

"Let's get moving." he continued.

Calum placed his water bottle down on the coffee table in his living room, he picked up a leather jacket from one of the sofas and made his way to the exit, stopping off for a few seconds to set his burglar alarm on a consul on his right hand side as he made his way along the main corridor in his house.

Calum closed the front door behind him and made his way over to his car that was parked in the centre of the driveway.

Brian was standing next to Calum's car. He was dressed in a black polo neck jersey, blue jeans and tan Timberland boots.

Calum approached the car and Brian and opened up the boot with his remote key fob. The front boot opened up a little and Calum manually opened it up the rest of the way and put his leather jacket inside.

"Ready?" inquired Brian.

"Ready." replied Calum as he closed the boot and opened up the car doors with the fob.

Both Calum and Brian got into Calum's car.

"Where's your car?" Calum asked Brian as he backed his car out of the driveway and drove away.

"It's parked a couple of streets over." replied Brian.

"OK" said Calum.

"I appreciate you sorting me out with a disposable car Calum. I don't want to use my own car for forensic reasons and I think your car wouldn't blend in in Craiglen." said Brian.

Brian had a point. If the cops were going to seriously look at him for these crimes they would probably get a warrant to examine his car. so it would be better to use another car for what he wanted to do and Calum's Porsche wouldn't really blend in in a fairly deprived area like Craiglen.

"So tell me about this guy we're going to meet." said Brian.

"Marco?" replied Calum.

"Marco is a good guy. A good egg," Calum continued.

"I've known Marco Carella all my life. We've been friends since we were children. His Dad was a friend of my Dad's and we used to hang around together as children." Calum continued further.

"Marco Carella?" asked Brian.

"Aye. Carella. He's half Italian on his Dad's side," said Calum.

"He runs a car chop shop based from a warehouse in Coatbridge. It's a little bit out the way but there's no CCTV in the industrial estate he works out of." Calum continued.

"Makes sense. Is he good at what he does?" asked Brian.

"The best. He learned his trade as a teenager on extended summer holidays with his Dad's family in Milan. His Mum and Dad, aunts and uncles all thought he was a good boy away playing football or hanging out at a local skate park with his cousins when him and his cousins were really away stealing Audis for one of the local crime gangs." replied Calum.

"Has he ever been caught?" asked Brian.

"Never. He just runs the chop shop these days stripping down and cannibalising cars. He has some very good and capable guys working for him and he prides himself as being probably the most technologically advanced car chop shop in the West of Scotland. He was the first to start using anti GPS. tracking hardware on the cars he has stolen. Skills and techniques he picked up from his cousins in Milan." said Calum.

"What kinds of cars does he usually steal or have stolen?"

asked Brian.

"He sticks to executive class cars. Audis, B.M.W.s, Mercedes' and Range Rovers. Nothing more upmarket like Porsches or Ferraris and nothing more downmarket like Fords or Vauxhalls. He's got a network extending across the whole of the U.K. in place to sell on the parts of the stolen cars. Wheels, interiors, engine parts and anything else worth selling on." said Calum.

The real money in stealing cars in Scotland was to be made from stripping cars down and selling the parts. There is not a big demand for stolen cars given fake IDs, known as ringed cars or ringers, because in Scotland and the rest of the U.K. the steering wheel was on the right while in North America and most of Europe the steering wheel is on the left.

"Do you trust him?" asked Brian.

"Absolutely. I'd trust him with my life." replied Calum.

"Good," said Brian.

"That's good," he continued.

"Its's sparky Adam's funeral tomorrow and I want to get close to the mourners at his wake at the Craigy Inn." Brian continued again.

Sparky Adams was the 4th guy Brian killed. The guy that got spiked through the heart a week ago in the Craigy Inn. The irony that the celebration of his life was to be held in the place that he died was not lost on Calum.

Twenty five minutes later Calum pulled his car into the entrance road of a fairly large warehouse of maybe 25,000 square feet with 6 separate lorry loading doors along the nearside of the building.

The entrance area consisted of a motorised barrier across the road manned by a security guard.

Calum stopped his car at the barrier and the security guard

wearing the uniform of the security company he worked for and a high vis vest with a radio clipped onto his belt came over to the driver side of the car.

"Can I help you?" asked the guard.

"I'm Calum McCulkin. I'm here to see Marco Carella. He's expecting me." said Calum.

Brian remained silent.

The guard took the radio off his belt and spoke into it.

"I've got a Calum McCulkin here to see Marco. He says Marco is expecting him." said the guard.

A few seconds later he got the reply.

"That's fine Alec. Send him in." said a male voice on the radio.

"Park anywhere you like. The entrance is the doorway in the middle of the building." said the guard pointing over to the doorway he was talking about before walking over and into his security hut and hitting the button for the barrier to rise.

The barrier rose up and Calum drove his car into the carpark area outside Marco's warehouse.

Calum reversed his car into an empty space opposite the entrance doorway and got out the car. Brian also got out the car. Calum opened the front boot of his car with his remote key, took out his leather jacket, put it on and started to walk towards the entrance closely followed by Brian.

Calum pushed open the entrance door and Brian and he walked into the warehouse to be greeted by Marco.

Marco Carella was 6 feet tall, average build with swept back jet black hair and could be described in Glaswegian terms as being a right handsome bastard meaning that he was very good looking probably due to his Mediterranean roots. He was dressed similarly to Calum in a nice suit and a shirt but no tie.

Of the large group of friends Calum had growing up Marco was by far the best at picking up women or pulling birds as it was known and it was an open ongoing joke amongst their friends that Marco had been in more holes than Tiger Woods.

Marco approached Calum with his arms outstretched to hug Calum. Calum reciprocated and reached out to hug Marco. Calum and Marco briefly hugged before Marco placed his hands on either side of Calum's face.

"It's been far too fucking long." said Marco.

"Aye. It's been a while." replied Calum.

"And who is this you've brought to meet me?" asked Marco.

"Marco this is Brian. Brian this is Marco." said Calum.

Marco and Brian shook hands.

"Any friend of Calum's is a friend of mine." said Marco.

"Good to know." said Brian.

Calum quickly glanced through the wide open space of Marco's warehouse. There were 4 cars parked in the warehouse in various stages of being stripped by guys too busy to even notice Calum and Brian were there.

There was a B.M.W. and a Mercedes and two other cars that Calum couldn't recognise as they were almost completely stripped down to the bare frameworks.

Marco ran a pretty efficient operation with most cars that they stole were brought into the warehouse and stripped down and cannibalised before their owners even knew they were missing.

The workplace was fairly noisy with the sound of various power tools getting used.

"I must admit I was surprised to hear from you looking for a disposable car. The last I heard you were mister squeaky clean. I heard you were working as a journalist." said

Marco.

"I am still working as a journalist. This is an exceptional case helping out a friend." replied Calum.

"That friend would be me." stated Brian.

"OK" said Marco.

"Do you have a toilet I can use?" asked Brian.

"Sure," said Marco.

"The very back of the building in the left hand corner. We'll wait here for you." Marco continued.

Brian walked away towards the left hand corner of the rear of the building.

"So who's the squaddie?" asked Marco.

"The squaddie?" asked Calum.

"Brian. Your mate. He's got that military swagger. I can recognise it from a mile away. He's either military or ex-military." said Marco.

Marco's intuition was always spot on.

He would've read Brian as soon as he walked through the door.

Calum paused for a second before answering.

"He's still in." said Calum.

"And he needs some help with some work he's got on?" asked Marco.

"Aye. He's got a score to settle and I'm going to help him." said Calum.

"Is it business or personal?" asked Marco.

"Definitely personal. It doesn't get more personal." replied Calum.

"I see." said Marco.

"Brian is the good guy in a horrible situation." said Calum.

"Enough said. I don't need to know the details. If you can vouch for this guy then that's good enough for me." said Marco.

"I can totally vouch for Brian. He's a good man. A good egg." said Calum.

"OK. That's good enough for me." said Marco.

By this time Brian had made his way back to where Calum and Marco were standing.

"All ready?" Marco asked Brian.

"Aye." replied Brain.

"Follow me." said Marco to Calum and Brian.

Marco lead Calum and Brian through his warehouse to a door at the far end. Marco opened the door that lead out to a small carpark at the rear of the warehouse.

"So Calum tells me you're looking for a disposable car that you can use for a few days Brian." said Marco as he opened the door.

"That's right." said Brian.

"Preferably something reliable that won't attract much attention. And something with a lot of boot space." Marco continued as he stepped out of the building and into the rear carpark.

"Aye." said Brian.

"Then I think I've got the very vehicle for you." said Marco pointing towards a black Audi Q5 parked in the carpark.

Brian walked over to the car and ran his hand along the side of it.

"It has a 2 litre petrol turbo engine with an automatic gearbox and it even has a full tank of fuel. Enough to last you a couple of days at least," said Marco.

"I've actually been using it to transport my guys between jobs as the registration plates are duplicates of another car parked up in long term parking area of Glasgow airport so the plates will not match with a car registered as being stolen," Marco continued.

"It's got a huge boot and I even had the windows tinted as

dark as I could so the driver of the car wouldn't get recorded on any CCTV. or speeding cameras. It's perfect for what I think you need mate." said Marco.

"It's perfect." said Brian.

"OK then." said Calum.

"How much?" he continued.

Marco smiled and exhaled deeply.

"Since you are an old friend and since you are planning to use it for something righteous I'll give it to you for what I paid the guys that acquired it for me. £350. That's the best I can do." said Marco.

"Deal." said Calum.

It was a very fair price in Calum's mind. He knew he'd get quoted mates rates but he didn't think it would be that cheap.

Marco reached into his trouser pocket, took out the remote locking key for the Audi and handed it to Brian.

"Here you go mate." said Marco.

"Thanks." said Brian.

Brian opened the door with the remote key and got into the driving seat. Marco stepped over to show Brian how to start the car up.

"There's a slot in the dashboard between the steering wheel and the radio. Put the key in there and push the start button beside it." explained Marco.

Brian did exactly as Marco said and the car started up.

"There's a button beside the handbrake that opens the boot." said Marco.

Brian quickly glanced down at the handbrake lever and noticed the boot release button.

"Got it." said Brian.

"If you drive down there to the left, the road will lead you out to the front of the building." said Marco pointing to the outside of the far end of the warehouse.

"I'll meet you round there Calum." said Brian as he started to drive the Audi off to the left.

"OK cool." replied Calum.

Marco held the door open for Calum as they both walked back into the warehouse.

Calum reached into his inside jacket pocket and took out an envelope full of cash as he walked beside Marco towards the main entrance door. Calum quickly counted through the cash until he reached £350 to pay Marco.

"Here you go." said Calum as he handed the money to Marco.

"Thanks." said Marco as he put the cash into his trouser pocket.

Less than a minute later Calum and Marco were approaching the main entrance door to the warehouse. Marco stopped walking and spoke to Calum.

"You do know that there's still a lot of respect for your family name don't you?" he asked Calum.

"I believe so." said Calum.

"There's people that would queue up to work with you if you wanted to get involved in anything criminal." Marco continued.

"I didn't know that." said Calum.

"I could introduce you to the right people for anything you wanted to get involved in. Drugs or guns, cars or girls. It would only take 2 or 3 phone calls at the most and I could set you up." said Marco.

"I'm flattered but not interested." said Calum.

"OK it's up to you." said Marco as he reached out to shake Calum's hand. Calum shook his hand and Marco pulled him closer.

"And don't leave it so long before you come and visit me

again." said Marco.

"I won't mate. I won't." said Calum as he opened the entrance door to the front car park.

"And Calum." Marco said loud enough to get Calum's attention as he walked out the door causing Calum to stop and turn around to face him.

"Aye?" asked Calum.

"Good luck with whatever it is you're up to with Brian." said Marco.

Calum smiled and gave Marco a thumbs up signal as he walked out the door towards the main carpark where his car was parked.

As soon as Calum walked outside the warehouse doorway he saw Brian parked alongside his car in the Audi with the engine running.

Calum walked over to the driver side of the Audi and tapped on the driver window to get Brian's attention.

Brian rolled down the window using the electric window switch on the driver door.

"So what do you think?" Calum asked Brian.

"It's perfect for what we need." Brian replied.

"I think we should park it up in my driveway. We don't want our stolen car getting stolen do we?" said Calum.

"What did you tell Marco about me?" asked Brian.

"I told him the truth. That you're the good guy in a terrible situation and that you had a score to settle." replied Calum.

"And that's it?" asked Brian.

"That's it" said Calum.

"OK. I'll drop the car off at your place then come back for it tomorrow morning about 9ish." said Brian.

"I'll see you then." said Calum.

Brian quickly turned the Audi around and drove towards the site entrance road with the barrier he and Calum had entered earlier.

Calum got in his car, started it up and followed Brian out of the carpark and then out of the industrial estate.

Calum placed his mobile phone into the cradle on the dashboard of his car and dialled Sarah's number.

The phone rang a few times before Sarah answered.

On the other end of the phone Sarah had just had a shower and was sitting on her bed with a white towel wrapped around her chest and another around her hair.

"Hello?" she asked as she held the phone to her ear.

"Hello Sarah. I just thought I'd check in with you in case you were worried about me." said Calum.

"Where are you?" she asked.

"I've just sorted our friend out with a new car and I'm on my way home. I'm fine." said Calum taking the precaution to not say too much in a mobile phone conversation.

"That's good. When can we meet?" asked Sarah.

"I'm busy with our friend tomorrow. What about Wednesday?" asked Calum.

Sarah paused for a few seconds before answering.

"OK that'll have to do," she started.

"Be careful Calum. Remember what Donny told you about guys like our friend. Remember what he said about blowing out candles." she continued taking Calum's lead in not saying too much over the phone.

"I'll be fine. There's no need to worry." said Calum calmly.

"I hope so Calum. I hope so." replied Sarah.

chapter eleven

Tuesday. 9.00am. West Glasgow

It was 9.00am in Calum's house in the West of Glasgow and Calum was sitting in his kitchen finishing off his breakfast cereal and coffee.
He was dressed in a smart suit and black tie because Brian had said he wanted to get close to the mourners at Sparky Adam's wake in the Craigy Inn later that day and he might need to blend in.
Calum took a drink of his coffee and looked at his watch and it was exactly 9.01am.
Calum picked up an iPad from the island in his kitchen and looked through the CCTV. live feed from the cameras on the front and the side of the house and he saw Brian walking up the driveway towards the Audi he and Calum purchased the night before. Calum's Porsche was parked alongside the Audi.
It was a fairly bright morning with no rain although it was still quite chilly with the occasional cold breeze.
Brian was dressed in jeans and a black polo neck jersey and was carrying a sports bag in his right hand. He opened the Audi using the remote key and got into the driver's seat then placed the sports bag in the front passenger seat.
Brian unzipped the bag and took out a large metal bracket not unlike the kind used for mobile phones but larger probably big enough for an iPad or another similarly sized hand held tablet computer.
Brian found the hinge on the back of the bracket and held

the plate part of the hinge up against the middle of the dashboard in the Audi with his left hand then reached into the bag again with his right this time taking out a red and black cordless drill and some 3 inch screws.

Brian placed the screws into his mouth then quickly placed the end of the drill onto the top left hand corner of the hinged plate and drilled through it into the dashboard. He quickly repeated the process 3 more times in the remaining corners of the hinged plate of the bracket.

Brian placed the bracket down on the top of the dashboard as he rummaged around inside the sports bag with both of his hands feeling around for something. After a few seconds he took out a drill bit key and a screwdriver bit for the drill.

Brian quickly loosened off the boring drill bit with the key and replaced it with the screwdriver bit he had just taken out the bag. He quickly tightened the screwdriver bit into place with his key and he was ready to continue.

Brian took the hinged frame off the top of the dashboard and placed the plate he had just drilled the holes into over the new holes on the front of the dashboard.

He took one of the screws out his mouth and pushed it into the top left hole of the plate over one of the holes he had just drilled. Once the screw was in place he quickly took the drill and screwed it into the dashboard.

Once the first screw was in place Brian quickly screwed the remaining 3 screws into place securing the bracket solidly into place.

Brian had fitted and used the piece of equipment he was fitting to the Audi many times in many vehicles in many countries. He had done it so many times he could probably be able to set it up while blindfolded.

Calum had seen Brian on the CCTV cameras and had

approached the Audi carrying and drinking from a coffee mug.

Calum stood silently for a few seconds beside the Audi before speaking to Brian.

"Can I get you something Brian? A cup of tea? Coffee? Mineral water? Asked Calum.

"No thanks I'm fine." said Brian leaning to one side reaching into the sports bag with both hands and taking out a Stingray phone tracker by the handle on each end of the device.

The Stingray phone tracker was a very powerful piece of surveillance kit for intercepting and monitoring mobile phones, text messages, emails and video calls. It could also activate the GPS. on most modern phones and track a phone in real time. All without the owner or the user of the phone having any idea he or she was being monitored.

The Stingray works by pretending to be a mobile telephone mast and allowing mobile phones in the vicinity to connect to it and pass all information through it. The Stingray itself also connects to real mobile telephone masts to pass the data on so the target phone user has no idea their information is being monitored in real time.

The device itself was a fairly innocuous looking metal box about the same size and shape as the average adult's shoe box with fifteen or so settings switches and buttons on the front as well as 2 U.S.B. ports, an Ethernet port and a 12 volt power connection plug specifically designed for use in motor vehicles.

The Stingray device itself doesn't have a user interface to display information or to type in commands. That has to be done via either a laptop or a tablet type device connected to the main device by an Ethernet cable. That was what the bracket Brian was attaching to the dashboard was for. It was for a tablet type device that came as part of the overall package.

Stingrays were originally intended to be used by militaries, intelligence / security services and top tier law enforcement agencies friendly to the United States but over the years other entities have managed to either procure Stingray kits or to reverse engineer them and produce their own versions of them. Pretty much every country in the World has Stingray or Stingray-like technology in use in their country although very few will openly admit it due to the nature of operating a Stingray device because it intercepts and monitors all mobile phone calls and operations within a certain radius without a warrant.

"Is that a Stingray?" asked Calum.

"Sure is." replied Brian.

"Do you know about Stingrays?" asked Brian as he took the charging and Ethernet cables out of the sports bag.

"Not really. I've heard them mentioned in conversations. That's about it. The last I heard they retailed at more than a hundred grand a piece." asked Calum.

"Aye. A hundred grand and all the rest." said Brian.

"How did you get your hands on one?" asked Calum.

"Well let's just say that you have mates that can help you out with some things and I've got mates that can help me out with others." said Brian.

"OK" said Calum.

Brian continued to plug in the Ethernet cable and the power cable into the Stingray before taking out a bespoke tablet computer and placing it into the bracket he had just attached to the dashboard.

Calum wondered where Brian had borrowed such an expensive device from. As a serving soldier in the SAS he would have colleagues in a lot of clandestine organisations

SAS/ MI5/ MI6/ GCHQ/ a private military contractor? Who knew?

Calum noticed Brian was casually dressed in jeans and a jersey and not in funeral attire.

"How close are you planning to get to Cloud and his mates at the wake?" asked Calum.

"Maybe 100 metres maybe slightly less." said Brian as he powered up the Stingray and the tablet control interface to give it a full system check.

"So I can get changed into something less formal?" asked Calum.

"Aye. Sure." replied Brian.

Calum walked away quickly to get changed into something more casual. As he walked away the plan to not get too close made perfect sense to him. Of course it would be a bad idea to mingle amongst the mourners at the funeral as he had already been involved in confrontations with Cloud, Razzy and the half dozen or so gang members present at the gang H.Q. when Calum laid hands on Razzy. He would definitely get recognised by some of the gang members and it would probably lead to an ugly scene.

A few minutes later Calum returned to Brian and the Audi in the driveway dressed casually in jeans, trainers and a grey hooded top. Calum was also holding an envelope in his right hand.

Brian was sitting in the driver's seat of the Audi and had just finishing up the systems check on the Stingray.

"Are we good to go?" asked Calum.

"We sure are." replied Brian.

"So now what? asked Calum.

"Now we wait," started Brian.

"Sparky's funeral service is at 11 so by the time the service is over and the burial has been performed it'll probably be

12 by the time they hit the pub and we'll be there waiting." said Brian.

Calum looked at his watch. It was almost 9.30.

"So we've got two and a half hours to go until then?" asked Calum.

"Aye. Is there something you need to do or somewhere you need to be?" asked Brian.

"There is actually. I'd like to check in with my work partner and let her know everything is OK and I need to post a letter." said Calum.

"OK. There's something I need to do as well. So we'll meet back here at half 11?" said Brian.

"Sounds good to me." said Calum.

Tuesday. 10am. South Glasgow.

Half an hour after the conversation with Brian in the driveway Calum was parked across the road from Sarah's place in the South of Glasgow. It was still quite bright but chilly outside. He was waiting for Sarah who he texted 20 minutes ago.

Out of the corner of his right eye he saw Sarah starting to make her way across the road towards him and his car.

A few seconds later she was getting into passenger seat in his car.

"Morning." she said as she sat down.

"Morning." replied Calum as he put the car in gear and drove off.

"I wasn't expecting to hear from you until tomorrow at the earliest. I thought you'd be busy with our friend." said Sarah.

"I've got a couple of hours before I'm needed so I thought I'd check in with you and let you know everything is OK." said Calum.

"And is everything OK?" asked Sarah.

"You don't have to go along with what he's planning you know. If you want out all you have to do is tell him." Sarah continued.

"I'm cool. I want to be involved in this." replied Calum.

"OK If you say so." said Sarah.

There was a brief pause as neither Calum or Sarah had anything to say.

"Is there anything I can do for you?" asked Sarah.

"Actually there is. I'd like you to put a stamp on and then post a letter for me." said Calum as he reached into the driver side door pocket and took out a sealed envelope then passed it to Sarah.

Sarah looked at the address on the envelope.

"Thomas McGurk. H.M.P. Barlinnie." Sarah said aloud.
"Where do I know that name from? McGurk?" she asked.
"It's the scary guy Sned is locked up with in the clink." replied Calum.
"And you are writing to him why?" asked Sarah.
"Because I want him to know what kind of guy Sned is. What he is and what he's done." said Calum calmly.
"And to what end? What are you hoping to get out of this?" Sarah asked.
"Nothing. Absolutely nothing." said Calum.
"And if this guy McGurk kills Sned are you going to get charged with conspiracy or aiding and abetting?" asked Sarah.
"No. There's nothing in that letter that requests, encourages or condones violence in any way. There's nothing that will land me in hot water. It's just one guy telling another guy what a third guy is all about. What he has been doing," stated Calum. He wasn't stupid and he had obviously thought about the wording of the letter in depth.
"The letter will be scanned for weapons and sniffed for drugs and if it isn't red flagged at either of these examinations the letter will be passed on to the inmate with no questions asked." explained Calum
Sarah paused before speaking again. She knew that if she didn't post it Calum would just post it himself so she decided to go along with it.
"OK" she said.
"I'll do it but I want to hear from you at least once a day every day until this whole Brian thing is over so I know you're still in one piece." she continued.
"Deal." said Calum.
"Is there anything else I can do?" asked Sarah.
Calum paused for a few seconds before answering.

"We really need to start working on our cover story. You've already told Bobby McCiver that the whole thing is a dispute between rival factions in the gang so we need to go with that." said Calum.

"We can do that but like I told you before that for that story to work there needs to be at least one surviving member to commit the last murder. We need to pin it on somebody." said Sarah.

"Don't worry about that I'm working on it." said Calum.

Tuesday. 11.15am. West Glasgow

Calum drove his car through his open gates and into his driveway to be greeted by Brian standing and leaning against the Audi.
It was a fairly sunny morning but still quite chilly in the shade.
Calum parked alongside the Audi and got out his car.
"Ready?" inquired Brian.
"Aye. Ready" replied Calum.
"OK let's do this." said Brian as he opened up the Audi with the remote key fob.
Brian got into the driver's seat and Calum started to get into the front passenger seat but paused when he noticed the Stingray was sitting in the flooring area of the seat and that it was plugged into the tablet in the bracket Brain was fitting earlier via an Ethernet cable and into the cigarette lighter via a power cable.
"Be careful with that," said Brian.
"You know how much it's worth." he continued.
Calum didn't know exactly how much the Stingray was worth but he did know that it was worth comfortably in excess of a hundred thousand pounds so he gently pushed it to the side before getting into the seat and putting his feet in the flooring area.
Calum closed the door behind him and Brian reversed back out of the driveway and onto the road outside.

Tuesday. 11.50am. North Glasgow

Brian parked up the black Audi Q5 with the blacked out windows approximately 80 metres along the road from the Craigy Inn.

The road he parked on was a busy main road with lots of traffic passing by and there were several other cars also parked on the road but he was happy that he had found a parking space with a direct uninterrupted view of the outside of the Craigy Inn.

"This will do us, perfect." said Brian as he parked the car.

"So what happens now?" asked Calum.

"Now we wait for Cloud to come outside and use his phone. Does he smoke?" asked Brian.

"I'm not sure. I've only spoke to him once for a couple of minutes on his doorstep. I think it's a safe bet that he likes a smoke of weed though as they all do." said Calum.

Brian reached into the back seat of the car, picked up the sports bag he was carrying earlier and placed it on the armrest between the two front seats.

"Time for you to get acquainted with the equipment you are going to be using." said Brian as he unzipped the bag.

Brian reached onto the bag and took out 2 pairs of binoculars, put one pair in his lap and handed Calum the other pair.

"Here's the binoculars you are going to be looking for Cloud with. They're pretty powerful and we use them all time in the regiment. Do you need me to show you how to use them?" asked Brian.

"No. I think I know how to use them." replied Calum.

"OK" said Brian as he reached into the bag again this time taking out a pair of headphones and a black metallic cylinder covered in black metal mesh.

Brian handed the cylinder and the headphones to Calum who took them from Brian.

The black cylinder was about the same size and shape as a Red Bull can but was pretty heavy for the size of it. Calum noticed a black plastic switch on one end of it.

"That's a military grade remote surveillance microphone used by intelligence and security agencies and special forces worldwide," said Brian.

"It has a range of maybe 200 metres so it should do fine for what we need it for. All you'll have to do is switch it on, roll down your window, position it outside the window and point it at whatever conversation you want to listen in on." Brian continued.

"Got it." said Calum.

"The headphones are paired to the microphone via Bluetooth. They'll link up as soon as you switch on the microphone." said Brian.

"OK" said Calum.

"When Cloud comes out and uses his phone you are going to listen into his conversation and report back to me everything that's said and I'll pair it up with the Stingray." said Brian.

"OK" said Calum again.

"And that's about it. Now we just wait for this little shit Cloud to put in an appearance." said Brian.

Brian reached into the sports bag again and brought out a paper folder.

"I've got a file on Cloud here if you're interested." said Brian as he reached over to hand it to Calum.

"But you probably won't need it. I'm sure you've got your own intel files and you obviously know what he looks like as you've already been to his door." said Brian.

Calum took the folder from Brian.

"I'll take a look at it." said Calum as he opened the folder to look inside.

The file Brian had in his possession was almost identical to the file Sarah had compiled on Cloud. It even had the same mugshot photograph. That suggested to Calum that Brian's intel files came from the same place Sarah's did. Police intelligence.

Calum quickly scanned through the document looking for something he didn't already know about Cloud but there was nothing new in the file. Criminal record, time served, current address and that's about it.

"There's nothing there I didn't already know." said Calum as he handed the folder back to Brian.

By the time Calum had finished with the folder Brian was already looking through his binoculars at the outside of the Craigy Inn.

Calum placed the folder onto Brian's lap and picked up his set of binoculars to take a look as well.

"Do you see anything interesting?" asked Calum.

"Nothing yet. I've seen a few people going in but nobody dressed for a funeral coming out for a smoke." said Brian.

"Give it a wee while. Maybe an hour." said Calum.

"Time to see what the Stingray is picking up." said Brian as he pushed the power button on the top edge of the tablet computer held in the bracket he had attached to the dashboard earlier that day. The Stingray was already switched on.

Calum couldn't see the display on the tablet computer because of the angle it was attached so he would just have to process whatever Brian told him.

The tablet computer started listing all the mobile phone signals it was picking up with the numbers scrolling on the display face of the tablet. Brian waited for the tablet to stop scrolling through the numbers.

"The Stingray is picking up a hundred and sixteen different mobile numbers in the radius with five of them currently in use," said Brian.

"We need to catch Cloud using his phone. If we can do that we should be able to easily sift through the list of phones getting used to find his." Brian continued.

"We will get him soon enough." said Calum.

There was a short pause before either of them spoke again.

"So tell me how you are going to get at that other bastard Sned in the prison." inquired Brian.

"I've wrote a letter to an old family friend that's locked up with him explaining exactly what Sned is and what he's done." said Calum.

"And what is this family friend's story?" asked Brian.

"McGurk? Tam McGurk is a scary guy. He's a six foot four and twenty five stone psychopath lifer with nothing to lose." said Calum.

"And you think he'll take out Sned just because of what Sned has done?" asked Brian.

"Probably. I'd say at the very least he'll have a word in Sned's ear." said Calum.

"A word in his ear? That sounds pretty mild" said Brian.

"Not really. If McGurk is involved then Sned's ear probably won't be attached to his head when McGurk has a word in it." said Calum.

"I see." said Brian.

"My Dad used to employ him sometimes to collect debts because nine times out of ten the guy that owed my Dad money would take one look at McGurk and pay up straight away. Like I said he's a scary guy." said Calum.

"And what happens if McGurk decides for whatever reason not to kill Sned?" asked Brian.

"I'll give him a week or two to make his move and if he doesn't kill him I'll reach out to McGurk and see how much money he wants to do it," said Calum as he looked through the binoculars again at the front of the Craigy Inn. "I just need to work out how to contact him as I'm barred from visiting anyone at Barlinnie, phone calls are recorded and letters can be intercepted. I could send my workmate Sarah to visit McGurk but I don't want to involve her. This is not her world and it never will be." said Calum.

"Why are you barred from Barlinnie visits?" asked Brian as he clearly didn't know what happened between Calum and Sned a few days previously.

"I assaulted Sned. Left him needing surgery and stitches." said Calum.

"And why did you assault him?" asked Brian already knowing the answer but he just wanted to hear it said aloud.

"Because he's a granny bashing junkie scumbag and a fucking waste of oxygen," replied Calum.

"Here we go," said Calum getting a little excited.

"That's the mourners starting to arrive." he continued.

Brian quickly picked up his binoculars and looked down the road towards the Craigy Inn.

Calum and Brian both watched as a group of 4 young men in suits and black ties walked towards the entrance of the pub from the other side of the building.

"Is he there?" asked Brian.

"Nope." said Calum.

"Do you recognise anyone?" asked Brian.

"Nah. I don't know any of them." said Calum putting his binoculars back down onto his lap.

The young men Calum and Brian saw were the first of the mourners to make it to the pub but many others would follow including their intended target Andy McLeod aka

Cloud.

"What exactly is the plan once we've got his mobile number? What happens next?" asked Calum.

"Once we've got his mobile number we can track him wherever he goes and we can take him out at a time and place of our choosing." said Brian.

"OK" said Calum.

"Here's some more mourners." said Brian watching them through his binoculars.

Calum quickly picked up his binoculars to look at the mourners crossing the road towards the Craigy Inn. There were 3 young men and 2 young women dressed in black. Cloud was not one of them.

"He's not there is he?" said Brian.

"Nope. Not yet. But he will be soon." replied Calum.

Just then the same dark blue Vauxhall Astra with a lowered suspension, tinted windows and a big bore exhaust, that Calum had seen Razzy and some other schemies getting out of the second time he spoke to Razzy at the gangs H.Q. slowly drove past the Audi Calum and Brian were sitting in. It was the booming bass of the car's sound system that initially got Calum's attention.

"I recognise that car. This could be him." said Calum.

Brian watched the car through his binoculars.

The car slowed down and then stopped outside the Craigy Inn and its passengers got out. One from the front and 3 from the back all dressed in black. Razzy got out the front passenger seat followed by 2 other young men Calum had never seen before, one from either side of the back seat and then Cloud got out. He had been sitting in the middle of the back seat.

All 4 passengers got out the Astra and Razzy bumped his fist on the roof of the car a couple of times to signal to the driver that he could go.

All 4 passengers from the Astra were all dressed in black for the funeral and they all made their way towards the bar area of the pub.

"That's him," said Calum.

"Second from the right." he continued.

Brian was already watching the group via his binoculars.

"Hello cunt." Brian said quietly.

As soon as Razzy, Cloud and the other 2 mourners entered the pub Calum and Brian both rested their binoculars in their laps.

"So now we know that he's definitely in the pub." said Calum.

"Yes" said Brian.

"How many different mobiles is the Stingray picking up?" asked Calum.

Brian quickly looked at the display tablet before answering.

"A hundred and twenty two with five currently in use. It would be like trying to find a needle in a haystack trying to pick out what number is Cloud's." said Brian.

"So now we just wait?" asked Calum.

"Yes. This is the reality of surveillance operations. It's about hours and hours of keeping an eye on a location waiting for a person of interest to show up. The toughest thing about it is staying awake." said Brian.

"But that shouldn't be an issue for us. We already know the guy we're looking for is in there. We're just waiting for him to pop outside for a smoke. It'll take us an hour or maybe two at the most." said Calum.

Brian reached into the sports bag in the back seat, pulled out a tube of green Pringles and took the plastic lid off.

"Let's hope it's not longer than that. I don't have enough Pringles to last much longer." said Brian as he held the open tube in front of Calum offering him some.

This was the first humorous comment Brian had made to Calum and it just went to show that Brian was totally at ease in the situation they were in. Brian had done this countless times before in neighbourhoods far more dangerous than Craiglen.

"Thanks." said Calum as he reached into the Pringles tube and took out a half dozen or so crisps.

"So what's life like in the SAS?" asked Calum.

"In a word. Busy," said Brian after he swallowed some crisps he was eating.

"These days I spend more time training foreign troops than anything else. There's always somebody somewhere wanting their troops to be taught by the S.A.S." said Brian.

"In any given year I might get posted to the Middle East, Africa, Asia or South America with no home leave." Brian continued.

"You must see a lot of the world. Do you ever miss Craiglen? I know you grew up here." commented Calum.

"I miss it like I'd miss a cancerous growth. If my Gran didn't live here I would never set foot in the place again." said Brian.

Brian paused for a few seconds before continuing.

"But that's not an issue now so I suppose I'll never be back after Cloud and Sned have been dealt with." said Brian.

Out of the corner of his eye Calum noticed movement down at the pub.

"There's movement at the pub." Calum said quickly as he put his binoculars to his eyes.

Brian did likewise.

Through their binoculars Calum and Brian could see that the movement at the pub was 5 young men all dressed in funeral attire entering the pub. Cloud was not one of them.

"He's not there." said Brian.
"No he's not. It's just more schemies attending the wake." Calum commented.
Calum and Brian both placed their binoculars down onto their laps.
A couple of minutes passed before either Calum or Brian spoke.
"Have you decided what you're going to do with Cloud's body? Do you need me to get you access to a blast furnace or a wood chipper?" asked Calum.
"No thanks. I'm just going to bury him in a forest in the middle of nowhere." said Brian.
"OK cool." said Calum.
Another couple of minutes passed before either Calum or Brian spoke.
"You should know that there's a good chance the police might interview you in the next week or two." said Calum.
"And why is that?" asked Brian.
"My workmate has been using the police intelligence computers to look into you. That's how we found you. And it's highly likely that every search she has done, every file she has looked at and everything she has printed off has been logged somewhere for the police to look through later." said Calum.
"OK" said Brian.
"I'd say you have a week or maybe two before they want to speak to you." said Calum.
"Good to know." said Brian.
"You need to make sure that there's nothing that can link you to the killings." said Calum.
"I know that." said Brian.
"I'm thinking about your car. Your Volkswagen Golf." said Calum.

"What about it?" asked Brian.

"Is there any chance there might be some forensic evidence in it? Some microscopic trace of blood or hair or skin? Some transfer from a weapon or a tool or a tied up body?" explained Calum.

Brian thought about what Calum had just said for a minute or so before answering.

"It's possible." Brian stated.

"Well you need to burn your car first chance you get." said Calum.

"I'll torch it as soon as I get back to Hereford." said Brian.

Brian noticed some activity outside the pub.

"Here we go." said Brian as he quickly raised his binoculars to his eyes and Calum also raised his binoculars to his eyes.

Down at the pub 2 schemies in suits and black ties stood next to each other and lit up cigarettes together. A few seconds later Razzy and Cloud walked out of the pub and joined the 2 schemies for a smoke.

"That's him on the left." stated Calum.

"Got him." said Brian.

Calum and Brian watched silently as Razzy, Cloud and the other 2 schemies smoked and chatted outside the pub.

Cloud reached into his inside pocket in his jacket, took out his phone and looked at the display screen.

"He's taking out his phone," said Calum.

"It looks like he's reading a text message." Calum continued.

"Come on cunt. Use your phone." Brian said calmly as he watched the group outside the pub through his binoculars.

Cloud held his phone in his left hand in front of his face and started typing onto it with his right.

"He's typing something onto his phone." said Calum while

Brian remained silent.

Cloud switched from holding his phone in his left to holding it with his right and put the phone against his right ear. It was what Calum and Brian had been waiting for. Cloud was making a call on his mobile phone.

"He's making a call." said Calum.

"OK. Get the microphone on him and repeat everything he says word for word and I'll pair it up with the Stingray intercepts." said Brian.

Calum quickly put on the headphones, switched on the microphone listening device Brian had given him earlier, rolled down his window and reached outside to rest the microphone on the passenger side mirrors with the device pointing towards the pub.

Brian also put on a smaller set of headphones matched up to the Stingray.

Cloud took a few steps away from Razzy and the 2 other mourners to speak on the phone. Calum adjusted the angle the microphone was positioned at to get the right angle.

"Here we go." said Calum.

"Remember I need it word for word." said Brian.

The phone number Cloud dialled rang 3 or 4 times before someone answered and Cloud began to speak with Calum repeating everything that Cloud said in the conversation to Brian who would match it up with the active use intercepts being picked up by the Stingray.

"Alright mate. How you doing? I got your message. What do you need?" Calum said to Brian.

"7 mobiles in active use. It's not either of the first 2." said Brian.

"Nah man I can't right now. I'm at Sparky's funeral. I can drop an ounce off later tonight if that's OK. About half 8ish?" Calum continued relaying everything Cloud said on the phone.

"Got him!" declared Brian.

"That's him right there with the number ending in 1-4-1-2." he continued while pointing to the display on the tablet interface for the Stingray.

Calum brought the microphone back into the car and put it and the headphones he was wearing down onto his lap.

"So what happens now?" asked Calum.

"Cloud is going to meet someone to make a delivery at half 8ish. We can park along the road from his house at about 8 o'clock and we can maybe pick him up when he makes his way to the meeting." said Brian as he started up the vehicle and started to drive away.

Brian was pleased that they had got Cloud's phone number stored in the Stingray. From now on they could listen in on his calls, read his text messages and even track his movements using the GPS. app on his smartphone.

Brian had Cloud exactly where he wanted him and Cloud had no idea about the situation he was in.

The way Brian was thinking at the time was that as far as he could tell Cloud didn't have a driving license so it was unlikely that he would be driving to the meeting and since all of his CYT mates would all be in the Craigy Inn drinking it was unlikely that any of them would be giving him a lift so he would probably be walking it.

At least that's what Brian was hoping.

Twenty five minutes later Brian was parking the Audi in Calum's driveway alongside Calum's Porsche. It was 1.20pm now and it was fairly sunny but chilly in the shade. Calum got out the Audi first followed by Brian.

"I'll meet you back here at twenty past 7." said Brian as he locked the Audi using the remote key fob.

"OK. Cool." said Calum.

Brian started to walk away down the driveway towards his car that he had parked a few streets away.

Calum walked over to his car, took out his phone, dialled Sarah's number and put the phone to his ear.

"Hello Sarah. What have you got planned for lunch?" he asked.

Tuesday. 2.10pm. West Glasgow.

Calum and Sarah were sitting down at opposite sides of a large circular dining table in Calum's Italian themed restaurant, Francesco's in Glasgow's trendy West End. The restaurant consisted of 14 large circular tables each approximately 5 feet in diameter and big enough to comfortably sit 6 people at each table.
Each table was covered in a white silk table cloth and all around the restaurant there were life-sized replica marble statues of various Christian and Greek deities.
Large but tasteful chandeliers hung from the ceiling and there was a bar area at the rear of the restaurant with waist high bar stools along the side of it.
The entire restaurant was busy with all of the dining tables filled to capacity and all of the bar stools were in use with people waiting for a table to become available.
Several suited waiters skilfully walked and weaved between the tables bringing food and drinks and bills to the customers.
Calum and Sarah were both eating the food that they had just ordered. Calum was eating Pappardelle with white bolognese and Sarah was eating sea urchin Spaghetti.
Calum had a bottle of mineral water and a half full glass in front of him while Sarah sipped from a large glass of Prosecco.
Calum had just finished telling Sarah about his afternoon with Brian.
Sarah held her right fist in front of her mouth until she had finished chewing her mouthful of food.
"And then what?" she asked.
Calum also finished chewing his food before answering.

"And then we went back to my place and parked up the Audi until we meet up again tonight." said Calum as he took a drink of water from his glass.

Sarah took a sip of her wine and leaned as far across the table she could without standing up to speak quietly to Calum.

"And you're sure you're OK with what's going to happen tonight with Cloud?" she asked.

"I'm fine with it. I see it as us just disposing of a piece of garbage." said Calum.

"OK," said Sarah leaning back into the sitting position in her chair.

"If you say you're fine with it then there's nothing more to discuss." she continued.

"Well actually there is. We need to get our cover story arranged." said Calum.

"I'm on it. But we need a survivor to blame the last public event on," said Sarah making sure not to use the word killing or murder in such a public area.

"We could do that. We can portray it as a tit for tat internal gang dispute but we need to make sure that he doesn't turn up in a month or two and destroy our narrative." said Sarah obviously talking about the possibility of Cloud's body being discovered and blowing a hole in the cover story she and Calum had concocted for the newspaper.

"Don't worry about it. He's going away tonight and he's never coming back." stated Calum to reassure Sarah.

"OK. If you say so." said Sarah.

"It is OK and I do say so." said Calum taking another drink of his water.

Tuesday. 3.30pm. South Glasgow.

Shortly after their lunch at Francesco's Calum was driving his car through Southern Glasgow to drop Sarah off at her flat. It was still fairly sunny but cold in the shade and Sarah had been silent all the way home.
"Are you alright?" asked Calum.
"Yes I'm fine." replied Sarah half-heartedly.
Calum could tell she was lying he just couldn't tell exactly what the issue was.
"Come on. I thought we were a team. What's up?" asked Calum.
Sarah remained silent for a few seconds pondering if she should tell Calum what was on her mind. In the end she decided she would tell Calum exactly what she was thinking.
"I'm just worried I'm not going to see you again. I'm afraid Brian is going to kill you when you've done this job together. I'm worried he's going to see you as a loose end that needs sorted." stated Sarah.
"That's not going to happen Sarah." said Calum tying to reassure her.
"How can you know that?" asked Sarah.
"You've only known this guy for a few days. How can you possibly know how this guy thinks and exactly what he is capable of? You heard what your mate Donny told you about guys like Brian. Killing someone is as easy blowing out a candle to them." Sarah continued.
"Brian is not a threat to me Sarah. I know it. I just know it." said Calum.
"Well I hope you're right Calum because you're gambling with your life. I hope you know that." said Sarah.

"I know that Sarah. I know that" said Calum again trying to reassure her.

Calum noticed that they were almost at the bus stop across from Sarah's place, that he always picked her up from and dropped her off at, coming up on the left hand side.

"That's us at your place." said Calum as he drove his car into the bus stop layby.

"So I suppose this is it." said Sarah.

"You're worrying about nothing Sarah. I'll text you when we're finished with this piece of shit Cloud." said Calum.

"Thanks. I'd appreciate that." replied Sarah as she unfastened her seat belt and started to get out the car.

"Sarah," Calum started.

"I'll be fine." Calum continued as Sarah got out the car.

"I hope so Calum. I really hope so." said Sarah as she closed the car door behind her.

Sarah stepped onto the pavement and watched Calum drive away into the distance then started to cross the road to her flat.

Tuesday. 7.15pm. West Glasgow.

Calum was pacing up and down in his kitchen, a large and fully equipped open-plan futuristic white marble effect area centred around a huge aluminium affect American style fridge freezer with a large island in the middle of the room. Calum held a small bottle of mineral water in one hand and an iPad in the other as he was watching his external CCTV. feeds from outside his house waiting for Brian to show up. He was dressed casually in the same jeans, trainers and a grey hooded top he was wearing earlier when they were watching the Craigy Inn.

As he paced back and forth he couldn't help but think about what Sarah had said and was concerned about.

Was she right?

As he had only known Brian for a few days could he really be sure Brian wasn't planning to kill him once they were finished with Cloud?

Calum's gut instinct told him that Brian wouldn't kill him after they had finished their business but was that feeling enough for him to be willing to bet his life on?

Calum took a drink from his water bottle and looked at the iPad in his hand where he saw Brian walking up the driveway towards the house carrying a spade, a green plastic petrol can and a set of bolt cutters.

Calum quickly gulped down the rest of the water in the bottle, put the empty bottle in his plastic recycling bin in his kitchen, placed the iPad down on the island in the kitchen and made his way to the front door to meet Brian. Calum quickly made his way through the house towards the front door, stopping at the burglar alarm control panel on the wall next to the door to quickly arm the alarm then opened the door and walked out onto the driveway to meet Brian.

As Calum walked out onto his driveway he saw Brian putting the spade, the petrol can and the bolt cutters into the boot of the Audi and approached him. Brian was dressed in jeans and a black polo neck jersey. The same way he was dressed for the surveillance work they did on the Craigy Inn earlier that day.

"Ready?" asked Brian.

"Yes." replied Calum.

"Are you sure?" asked Brian.

"This kind of work is not for everyone. If you want to back out, now is the time to say something. I can carry on without you. It'll be more difficult but I can manage." Brian continued.

"I'm fine. I'm good." replied Calum.

"Glad to hear it." said Brian as he put his hand on Calum's shoulder.

Brian opened the Audi doors with the key fob.

"So let's do this." he said as he got into the driver's seat in the vehicle.

Calum made his way around the vehicle and got in the front passenger's seat.

Tuesday. 7.50pm. North Glasgow.

Half an hour after meeting up in Calum's driveway, Calum and Brian were parked up in Burns Street in Craiglen about 80 metres along the road from Cloud's parent's house at number 39.

The road they were parked on was long and straight with run down houses on either side and each house had its own front space of maybe 20 square metres of concrete or slabs and a fence separating each space from their neighbour's. There was very little greenery in Craiglen. Trees, hedges and gardens were pretty scarce. It was just stone and concrete everywhere.

The view they had of the house Cloud was in was almost unobstructed because of the other vehicles parked in the street but that was not an issue as they didn't need a direct line of sight on him as the plan was to listen into Cloud's conversations in real time, to track him using the GPS. capabilities of his smartphone and not eavesdrop using a microphone that needed line-of-sight like they did earlier that day.

"Turn the Stingray on Calum. It's a wee black switch on the bottom right of the main face" said Brian as he powered up the tablet computer interface attached to the dashboard. Calum reached down into the foot well of the car and turned the Stingray so it was facing up the way. Just like Brian said there was a small black switch in the bottom right corner marked "power".

Calum flicked the switch then carefully placed the Stingray back down into its original position in the front passenger side foot well in the Audi.

The Stingray and its control panel interface sprung to life.

"Here we go." said Brian as he watched all the information being displayed on the tablet interface as the Stingray booted up.

Calum couldn't see the information on the tablet interface because of the angle it was attached to the dashboard facing the drivers position.

"OK cunt let's see if you've got your phone switched on." said Brian as he scrolled through the various options the Stingray offered on the tablet interface until he found the option to scan for a specific phone number already stored on the device.

Brian pressed the option to scan for Cloud's number on the interface and it almost instantly showed the results of the search. The Stingray was picking up Cloud's number with a signal strength of 5 out of 5. A very strong signal.

"Excellent," said Brian.

"Now we'll activate the microphone on his phone," said Brian as he tapped on the tablet interface.

"And now we'll activate the GPS. on his phone and we'll have him." Brian continued.

Brian tapped on the tablet interface a few times to activate Cloud's GPS. This was an operation he had done many times in different countries on several different continents. The commentary was purely for Calum's benefit so he knew what was going on.

"Activating GPS. in 3, 2, 1 seconds. GPS. activated." proclaimed Brian.

The user interface on the tablet had changed to a map detailing the local area and a circular icon on a house further along the street on the right. Cloud's parent's house.

"Got you you piece of shit." said Brian.

A couple of minutes passed until Calum spoke up.

"So how do you see this going down when it happens?" he asked Brian.

"I've got a dog leash and a syringe full of tranquillisers in that sports bag in the back seat. As soon as I get a chance I'll walk up to him asking about a lost dog and when I get close enough to him I'll just inject him full of tranquillisers. Meanwhile you can open the boot while I cable tie his wrists and ankles together and carry him over." said Brian.

"And then what?" asked Calum.

"And then we drive to your place so I can disconnect the Stingray and put it in your car then you can follow me to a spot I've got picked out to bury this piece of shit. We'll burn out this car and take your car home." Brian answered.

It was a sound plan but something bothered Calum.

"And you are sure no-one will witness you injecting then carrying Cloud over to this car?" he asked.

Brian smiled before answering.

"This is Craiglen Glasgow Calum. No-one ever sees anything. You should know that," said Brian.

"But just to be sure I'll wear my ski mask rolled up onto my head when I approach him then roll it down to cover my face when I inject him and carry him over here. The chances of someone witnessing me leaving this car and approaching Cloud and paying enough attention to give an accurate description to the cops is pretty small." Brian continued.

"Aye. You're right" said Calum nodding his head in agreement. Brian's plan was pretty good. Not perfect. But pretty good. Plans to commit any crime were never perfect. There was always an element of risk.

The Stingray control interface tablet started making rustling noises and it got both Calum and Brian's attention.

"I know that noise. He's putting his phone into his pocket. He must be getting ready to make a move." said Brian.
The Stingray had activated the microphone on Cloud's phone and was picking up every noise in the close vicinity of Cloud.
"I'm going out for a wee while mum. I won't be long." said Cloud's voice over the stingray.
"Where are you going?" said Cloud's mum's voice over the Stingray.
"I'm going down to see wee Sandy Miller about something. I shouldn't be long." said Cloud's voice over the Stingray.
"OK." said Cloud's mum's voice.
Just then the same dark blue Vauxhall Astra with a lowered suspension, tinted windows and a big bore exhaust, that Calum and Sarah saw Razzy getting out of at the CYT headquarters and that Calum and Brian saw Razzy, Cloud and the other mourners they were travelling with get out and walk into the Craigy Inn earlier, drove past slowly. Calum and Brian could hear the thump thump thump of a techno track being played at high volume through the sound system in the Astra before they actually saw the car. The Astra drove slowly past the Audi Brian and Calum were sitting in and stopped outside Cloud's mum's house.
"What's happening here?" asked Brian.
The tablet display for the Stingray lit up.
"He's got an incoming call." said Brian.
Cloud answered the call with Calum and Brian listening in.
"That's me outside Cloud." said Tosh's voice over the Stingray.
"OK I'll be right out mate." said Cloud.
"Fuck. He's getting a lift." spat out Brian angrily as he watched the GPS. tracker icon on the Stingray slowly move from the house towards the road that the car was parked on.

Brian glanced over his shoulder to the sports bag in the back seat. He still had the Glock pistol and the ski-mask he wore when he broke into Calum's house and it would be easy to just put on the mask and run over to the car and shoot Cloud twice in the head and once in the chest. What stopped him was what Calum said about trying to keep a low profile to avoid more police attention so he decided not to. He would just follow Cloud to wherever he was going and make plans from there.

The Astra was being driven by Tosh as Tosh didn't drink alcohol for medical reasons. He had chronic kidney problems like his father before him and his grandfather before him and was advised by his doctor to never drink alcohol and aggravate the condition, so he was allocated the position of CYT driver for Razzy and whoever Razzy wanted driven around.

Brian watched the GPS. tracker icon on the Stingray control interface tablet approach the road and pause for a second, as Cloud got into the car and listened as Tosh lowered the volume of the sound system in the car so he and Cloud could talk. then watched the GPS. tracker icon move as the car drove away.

Brian started up the Audi and drove off following the GPS. tracker on the tablet.

Following Cloud was easy because of the GPS. tracker. Cloud's exact location was displayed on a map on the Stingray user interface tablet. Brian didn't need to remain close enough to observe where he was going. He could afford to remain a hundred or even two hundred metres behind the Astra.

Brian and Calum listened in as Cloud and Tosh talked.
"Alright man. How are you doing?" asked Tosh.
"I've been better mate. I've been better." replied Cloud.

"Razzy told me to take you wherever you want to go and not to let you walk anywhere." said Tosh.
"That's cool mate. I'm just going to drop off a bit of weed at wee Sandy Miller's place and then back home again." said Cloud.
"Where does wee Sandy live?" asked Tosh.
"He's got a flat in Shaw Way. I'll show you the way." said Cloud.
"OK." said Tosh.
Shaw Way was at the other end of Craiglen but it was only a few minutes away in a car.
"Take the next right then the second left." said Cloud pointing the route out in front of Tosh.
Tosh complied and took the next right then the second left in his car.
"Now drive right to the end of the cul-de-sac." said Cloud.
The part of Shaw Way Cloud and Tosh were visiting was a cul-de-sac. A dead end road.
 "He's driving into a cul-de-sac. I can't follow him in without getting spotted. I'll park in the street next to where he's parked up." said Brian.
"OK." said Calum.
Brian drove past the entrance to the Shaw Way cul-de-sac and parked in the street next to it.
Tosh drove to the far end of the cul-de-sac past numerous parked cars and stopped his car.
Cloud got out of Tosh's car and walked towards the main entrance to the block of five storey high flats that Sandy Miller lived in.
Cloud reached the entrance to the flats and pressed the intercom button for flat 10. The intercom made a buzzing sound for a few seconds then Sandy's voice spoke over the intercom.

"Hello?" said Sandy's voice.
"Sandy it's Cloud. I've got your gear." said Cloud into the intercom.
"Ideal. Come on in." said Sandy's voice as the entrance door clicked open.
Brian and Calum could hear everything getting said and everything that happened via the microphone on Cloud's phone. They listened as the door opened, they listened in as he climbed the stairs to the top storey flat that Sandy lived in and they listened as he rang Sandy's doorbell.
Sandy Miller was a school friend of Cloud but had taken a different route to him in their teens. While Cloud was hanging around with Razzy and the rest of the CYT getting drunk and high and committing all kinds of petty crime every day and night Sandy was learning how to become an electrician and now held down a pretty good paying job with a legitimate electrical contractor company based in the East of Glasgow.
Sandy was just a wee guy at about five foot three and slimly built with short red hair and unlike most of the CYT Sandy had a job, a car and a house that he actually lived in and didn't just get used as a hangout for the gang members. Although he never really hung around with the CYT much he knew all of them and they all knew him. He was well liked by all of the CYT
Sandy answered the door to Cloud.
"Come in mate. Come in." he gestured to Cloud.
Cloud stepped through the doorway and into Sandy's house. He had been in Sandy's house many times as Sandy was a regular customer for weed. He probably came to Sandy's place once or twice a week every week with a weed delivery.
"Just go through. You know the way." said Sandy.

Cloud walked along the hallway into the living room and sat down sat down in the middle of Sandy's 3-seater black leather couch. Another 2 single seater black leather chairs were at either end of the room with a large flat screen television attached to the wall in the middle of the room. Cloud reached into his front jeans pocket and took out a ball of silver paper with the ounce of weed wrapped up in it.
Sandy entered the room and sat down in the chair on the right of where Cloud was sitting.
 "There you go mate." said Cloud as he reached over to Sandy and handed him the ball of silver paper with the weed in it.
Sandy immediately reached into his back pocket, took out his wallet and took out two twenties and a tenner and handed the money to Cloud.
"Cheers mate." said Cloud as he slid the money into his back pocket.
Sandy carefully unravelled the ball of silver paper and opened it up to reveal the weed.
Sandy held the silver paper and the weed up to his nose and inhaled deeply through his nose.
"I fucking love the smell of good weed." said Sandy smiling.
Cloud stood up to leave.
"I need to go. I've got Tosh waiting for me outside in his car." said Cloud.
"Woah. Woah. Woah," said Sandy.
"Are you leaving already?" he asked.
"I was hoping you'd stay for a wee while for a wee smoke and a drink. I've got a bottle of Smirnoff in the fridge chilling and I've got the Blu-ray collector's edition of 'Pink Floyd The Wall' ready to watch with my surround sound

TV. set up." Sandy continued.

"I… I… I…" Cloud stuttered.

"Come on. Live a little. You can get Tosh to pick you up later after the film." said Sandy.

"OK you win." said Cloud as he sat back down on the couch and took his mobile phone out of his jeans pocket and dialled Tosh's number. Tosh quickly answered his phone and Brian and Callum listened in to the ensuing conversation.

"Hello Tosh. Listen mate. I'm going to stay here for a wee while. I'm going to have a wee smoke and a drink with Sandy. I'll phone you when I need you. Probably in about 2 hours." said Cloud.

"OK mate. No problem." said Tosh before ending the conversation then reversing his car out of the cul-de-sac and driving away.

"Looks like we're going to be here for a while." said Brian as he reached into the sports bag in the back seat and took out a green tube of Pringles. Brian quickly took of the lid to the crisps and offered some to Calum.

"Thanks." said Calum as he took a few of the crisps out of the tube and put them in his mouth.

Brian also took a few crisps out of the tube and put them in his mouth.

Back in Sandy's flat Cloud was sitting on the couch and had just finished rolling a joint while Sandy had poured himself and Cloud a glass of Vodka and cola in the kitchen and was bringing them through to the living room.

Cloud reached over to the small glass coffee table in the centre of the room and picked up an ashtray as he put the joint in his mouth and lit it up.

Sandy placed both glasses of Vodka onto the coffee table and walked over to the television and DVD player in the corner of the room.

"So how did Sparky's funeral go then?" asked Sandy as he kneeled down in front of the TV to put the Blu-ray disc into the DVD player.

"Fucking awful mate. Awful" said Cloud exhaling smoke as he spoke.

"Still no idea who killed Sparky or any of the others yet?" asked Sandy as he picked up the DVD player remote from the coffee table as he walked past it to sit down on his seat.

"Nah man nobody's got any idea." said Cloud inhaling deeply from the joint in his hand.

"I had a daft newspaper reporter at my door on Friday telling me my life was in danger and that I should hand myself into the cops and confess to a crime they aren't even investigating. He said he could help me out with the threat to my life if I did." said Cloud exhaling again.

Sandy took a swig from his glass.

"I take it you told this reporter where to go?" asked Sandy.

"I certainly did. I tore up his business card in half and threw it back in his face and told him to go fuck himself!" said Cloud proudly as he passed the joint to Sandy.

"Cool." said Sandy as he took inhaled deeply on the joint.

"The thing is this fucking reporter also spoke to Razzy and Razzy thinks there might be something in what he's talking about." explained Cloud.

"Really?" asked Sandy.

"Aye really. That's why he's got Tosh driving me from place to place. He doesn't want me walking anywhere by myself like I'm a fucking child that needs looking after." said Cloud as he reached over to the coffee table and picked up his glass of Vodka and cola.

Sandy pressed the start button on the DVD player remote control and the television sprung to life with the opening credits for the feature film 'Pink Floyd The Wall'.

"Anyway I don't want to talk about this depressing shit. I just want to have a smoke and a drink and to chill out to some classic Pink Floyd." said Cloud.

"Amen to that brother." replied Sandy as he inhaled deeply on the joint.

"Enjoy the movie cunt. It might be the last one you ever see" said Brian outside in the Audi while Calum fiddled with his phone.

"I've just looked up the info for 'Pink Floyd The Wall' on the internet and it says it's 1 hour and 35 minutes long." said Calum.

Brian looked at the clock on the dashboard before replying. The time was exactly 8.12pm.

"So the film should finish at about 9.45?" said Brian.

"Aye. There or thereabouts." replied Calum.

Tuesday. 9.45pm. North Glasgow.

It was now 9.45pm in Craiglen, North Glasgow and Brian and Calum were parked up in their Audi Q5 a street over from the cul-de-sac Sandy Miller lived in and where Cloud was located.

Brian was in the driver's seat tapping his fingers on the steering wheel in anticipation as his adrenaline was starting to pump through his veins. He knew that in the next few minutes he would find out if he was going to get a chance to get at Cloud.

Both Brian and Calum were listening in on the goings on inside Sandy's flat via the microphone on Cloud's smartphone that they had hacked using the Stingray device Brian had borrowed from someone.

Inside Sandy's flat the credits were rolling for the end of 'Pink Floyd The Wall', a favourite film amongst weed smokers.

Cloud stood up from the couch he was sitting on and took out his phone.

"OK I need to get going." he stated to Sandy.

"Here we go." said Brian leaning in closer to the Stingray user interface to listen carefully to everything that was about to be said.

Cloud selected Tosh's number on his phone and hit the dial button. Tosh's phone rang and rang and rang eventually skipping onto the voicemail messaging service.

"Fuck!" said Cloud as he paused for a few seconds then tried Tosh's number again.

What Cloud didn't know was that at the other end of Craiglen, Tosh was in the back of a traffic cop car getting breathalysed as part of a random stop by the traffic cops and his phone was on a cradle attached to the dashboard in his car. Tosh's phone rang and rang but no-one could hear or answer it.

There was nothing random about Tosh getting stopped and breathalysed by the traffic cops. The cops knew he was in the CYT and they knew the CYT had a funeral and a wake that day so there would be a good chance that any CYT members driving that day would be driving drunk and that's why they stopped him. They didn't know about his health issues that prevented him from ever drinking alcohol.

Tosh was totally relaxed in the back of the traffic cops Volvo V70 estate as everything about the car was legal. Tosh held a full valid driving licence, the car was road taxed, it had a current M.O.T. certificate, it was insured and his tyres all had plenty of tread on them.

Tosh sat in the middle of the back seat of the car with a traffic cop in both the driver seat and the front passenger seat.

"Now then Thomas… do you mind if I call you Thomas?" asked the traffic cop in the driver seat.

"Only my mum calls me Thomas. Most people call me Tosh." Tosh replied.

"OK then is it OK for me to call you Tosh?" asked the traffic cop in the driver seat.

"Aye man. No problem." said Tosh.

"OK then Tosh under the Road Traffic Act Scotland 1988, I am asking you to provide us with a breath sample to check your blood alcohol count. Do you agree to give us a breath sample?" asked the traffic cop in the driver seat.

"Aye." said Tosh.

"Excellent." said the traffic cop in the driver seat as he reached backwards between the front car seats towards Tosh with the breathalyser instrument in his hand. The instrument basically looked like a calculator with a thick plastic tube attached to the top.

"Have you done a breathalyser test before?" asked the traffic cop in the driver seat.

"Aye. A few times. You need me to blow hard into the tube until you tell me to stop." said Tosh.

"That's right Tosh. That's right." said the traffic cop in the driver seat as he held the breathalyser device up to Tosh's mouth.

Tosh blew hard into the device until the traffic cop in the driver seat told him to stop.

"That's enough." said the traffic cop in the driver seat as he leaned back into his seat with the breathalyser device in front of him.

"We'll just give it a few seconds. Sometimes it doesn't register straight away." said traffic cop in the driver seat.

A few seconds passed before the traffic cop in the driver seat spoke again.

"Your breathalyser test has come back with blood alcohol count of zero." said the traffic cop in the driver seat.

"I could have told you that," said Tosh.

"I can't drink alcohol for medical reasons. I never touch the stuff." he continued.

"OK well we'll just do a quick persons check to see if you have any warrants out against you then you'll be free to go. It'll just take a couple of minutes as long as you don't have any warrants issued against you. You don't have any warrants out do you Tosh?" said the traffic cop in the driver seat.

"No mate I'm a good boy." said Tosh smiling.

Cloud tried Tosh's phone a third and then a fourth time and it just rang and rang and went onto the voicemail option.

"Fuck!" spat out Cloud.

"He's not answering his phone." Cloud continued.

"Do you want me to order you a taxi?" asked Sandy.
"Nah mate. Fuck that. I'll just walk it." Cloud replied.
"Yes!" proclaimed Brian as he clenched his fists excitedly.
"That's right cunt you should walk it." Brian continued.
"Are you sure that's a good idea?" asked Sandy.
"Razzy doesn't want you walking anywhere by yourself." Sandy continued.
"I'll be fine. I'm a grown man. I can take care of myself." replied Cloud.
"That's right cunt you are a grown man and you should walk home." said Brian.
"Have you got a blade I can borrow?" Cloud asked Sandy.
"A blade?" asked Sandy.
"Aye. A blade. A knife. The bigger the better." said Cloud.
"I've got the very thing." said Sandy before rushing away to the cupboard in his bedroom only to reappear a few seconds later with a large hunting knife in a sheath.
Sandy handed the sheathed knife to Cloud.
Cloud removed the knife from its sheath and looked at the blade. It was a 10 inch hunting knife with a blade down one side and a serrated edge down the other.
"That's my fishing knife. Try not to lose it," said Sandy.
"It's big enough to cut down branches off trees but still sharp enough to gut a fish." Sandy continued.
"Ideal." said Cloud.
Cloud stood admiring the knife for a few seconds before speaking.
"OK then I'll get going. Phone or text me when you need more weed." said Cloud as he tucked the sheathed knife down the back of his trousers.
"Will do mate. Will do. Just be careful on the way home." said Sandy.
"Don't worry about me mate. If anyone gives me any shit

I'll just fucking rip them wide open." said Cloud.

"That's what you think cunt." said Brian.

Brian and Calum listened in to everything that was being said until Brian pressed the button on the Stingray interface tablet to show only the GPS. location of Cloud's phone. Brian quickly scanned the GPS. map on the tablet to work out what route Cloud would take home and where would be the best place to intercept him. This was something Brian had done many times in many countries so he knew exactly what he was doing.

"Here!" proclaimed Brian touching a point on the Stingray display interface.

"I'll pick him up here." Brian continued as he started up the car and began to reverse out of the cul-de-sac he had parked the car in.

"Get that sports bag from the back seat for me mate." said Brian as he quickly steered the car through the back streets of Craiglen towards the point he was going to intercept Cloud.

Calum quickly got the bag out of the back seat and put it onto his lap.

"Open it up and take out some plastic cable ties. Just 2 or 3 will do." said Brian.

Calum put his hand into the bag and pulled out a half dozen or so black plastic cable ties.

"Got them." said Calum.

Good. Place them in your lap and now you're looking for a small metal case about the size of a cigarette packet." Brian continued.

Calum rummaged around in the bag until he found a metal case about the same size as a cigarette packet.

"Is this it?" asked Calum holding the case out in front of him.

"That's it" said Brian.
Calum put the case in his lap beside the cable ties.
"Now dig out a heavy rope dog leash." Brian continued.
"A dog leash?" asked Calum just making sure he heard Brain correctly.
"Aye. A dog leash." said Brian.
Calum put his hand into the bag again and rummaged around looking for a heavy rope dog leash that he found after a few seconds.
"Got it." said Calum as he held the leash in front of him.
"Excellent." said Brian as he parked the car at the location where he was going to intercept Cloud.
Brian took the cable ties out of Calum's lap and put them in his back pocket. He then picked up the small metal case and opened it up. Inside the case was a small hypodermic syringe held in place with protective foam.
Brian held the syringe in front of his face for a few seconds to look at the green liquid inside.
"What's that?" asked Calum.
"That's a liquid cosh." said Brian.
Calum had heard the term liquid cosh before. It originated from psychiatric facilities from whenever a patient was getting violent, to the point that he or she was a real physical threat to themselves or others, then that patient would get the liquid cosh. A cosh was street slang for baton or truncheon and the liquid cosh was a medication that would instantly knock someone out for a few hours.
There were many variations of the liquid cosh but they always consist of at least one heavy duty anti-psychotic and another heavy duty sedative. Enough to knock an adult out for few hours.
At the other end of Craiglen, Tosh was finished with the police and was getting back into his car. He sat down into

the driver's seat and immediately looked at his phone in the cradle on the dashboard and noticed that he had 6 unanswered calls from Cloud.

"Shit!" Tosh said out loud as he quickly took his phone out of the cradle and dialled Cloud's number.

Inside Calum and Brian's stolen Audi the Stingray display interface lit up displaying the details of an incoming call to Cloud's phone.

"Someone's phoning him." said Brian.

Cloud was on foot just around the corner from Sandy's house when his phone rang.

Brian and Calum could see exactly where he was, he was about 50 metres along the road from where they were parked and he was walking towards them and they could listen in to his telephone conversation.

Cloud answered his phone.

"Well well well if it isn't the most unreliable taxi driver in Craiglen." Cloud joked.

"I'm really sorry mate. I got stopped by the traffic cops. I couldn't answer my phone." offered Tosh.

"Don't worry about it mate. I'm just going to walk it." said Cloud.

"What? No!" said Tosh.

"What do you mean no?" asked Cloud.

"Tell me exactly where you are and I'll come and pick you up." said Tosh.

"I'll be fine mate. I'll be fine." said Cloud.

"Please Cloud. Tell me where you are so I can pick you up. Please Cloud." said an increasingly worried Tosh.

"OK OK," said Cloud

"I'm at the top of Harris Avenue." said Cloud.

"Stay exactly where you are. I'll be there in 3 minutes." said Tosh hurriedly.

"Fuck." spat out Brian.

If he was going to make a move on Cloud he was going to have to do it immediately before Tosh arrived.

"OK Calum. I'm going to make a move on Cloud. You sit here and wait for me to whistle as a signal that I've got him. When you hear me whistle I want you to get into the driver seat and release the boot for me to put him in." said Brian.

"OK. Got it." said Calum.

"Give me the dog leash." said Brian with his hand opened up to receive the rope leash.

Calum placed the leash into Brian's hand. Tosh and Cloud's telephone conversation continued with Calum listening in.

"Keep talking to me Cloud. What was wee Sandy saying to it?" asked Tosh just to start a conversation. Tosh had his phone in its cradle attached to his dashboard and was driving erratically to Cloud's location.

Brian approached Cloud with the dog leash in his left hand and the liquid cosh syringe in his right hand held behind his back.

"He wasn't saying much mate. We just had a wee drink and a smoke and that's about it." said Cloud.

"Have you seen my dog mate?" asked Brian.

"No mate I haven't seen any dogs." replied Cloud.

Brian took a few steps closer to Cloud. Cloud noticed that and quickly put his phone into his left hand and slowly put his right hand around to his back ready to pull out the hunting knife Sandy gave him.

"Who's that you're talking to?" asked Tosh.

"Just some random guy looking for a dog." said Cloud.

"Are you sure you haven't seen him? He's a white Staffie with a brown patch over his right eye. He's called Hector."

said Brian walking up to Cloud.

"Look mate. I told you I haven't seen him." said Cloud.

"And you never will." said Brian as he quickly lunged towards Cloud injecting him in the neck with the liquid cosh with his right hand and grabbing Cloud's right hand with his left to prevent Cloud from pulling out the hunting knife Brian knew he was carrying.

The liquid cosh took effect quickly with Cloud's eyes rolling back into his head and he collapsed into a heap on the footpath.

Brian picked up Cloud's phone that he dropped, looked at it for a couple of seconds and noticed that the display said he was still in a conversation with Tosh.

"Cloud? Cloud? Cloud?" Tosh shouted down the phone at Cloud.

Brian took a few steps back down the path, and quickly put the phone down a street drain that he noticed when he approached Cloud, then stepped back to Cloud's unconscious body.

Brian reached into his back pocket and took out 2 black plastic cable ties. He rolled Cloud onto his stomach and pulled his arms around his back then cable tied his wrists together then did the same with his ankles.

Brian then crouched down next to Cloud and proceeded to pick him up and sling him over his shoulder and started to walk back to the Audi Calum was waiting in.

Picking up a fully unconscious body from ground level is not as easy as it sounds. Thankfully Brian had a lifetime of experience picking up limp bodies in military training and during real firefight situations so it wasn't a problem for him.

Brian took a few steps onto the road and let out a loud whistle to alert Calum that he was coming with Cloud's unconscious body.

Calum heard Brian's signal and immediately got out the front passenger side door, quickly walked to the rear of the car, hit the boot release button, got into the driver door and started the car engine up.

The boot of the Audi opened slowly and fully automatically when the boot release handle was pulled and was perfectly timed for Brian arriving with the unconscious body.

Brian quickly tipped Cloud's unconscious body into the boot of the Audi with Cloud left lying on his right hand side with his back facing the boot. The boot was almost empty apart from green plastic petrol can full of petrol, the spade and bolt cutters Brian had bought earlier on that day. Brian then pulled up the back of Cloud's jacket to get at the knife he knew Cloud was carrying.

Brian found the sheathed knife tucked into the back of Cloud's jeans, removed it and closed the boot door before getting into the front passenger door.

"Go!" Brian said quickly.

Calum started to drive the car out of the spot it was parked at but stopped because of a car slowly approaching from behind.

As soon as Calum and Brian heard the sound of a big bore exhaust from the car they both knew who it was. It was Tosh coming to pick up Cloud and to take him home.

"It's Tosh." said Calum.

Tosh's car passed the car Calum and Brian were in slowly as Tosh carefully scanned the surrounding area for Cloud before parking his car up 50 metres or so along the road near where Brian had abducted Cloud.

Calum calmly drove the Audi out of the parking spot and away from that area of Craiglen watching Tosh in his car via the rear view mirror in the Audi.

Back in Tosh's car, Tosh was getting increasingly anxious about Cloud's whereabouts as he kept trying to phone Cloud but Cloud's phone just automatically kept going onto the voicemail option because his phone was submerged in water down the drain Brian put it down.
Tosh didn't know about Cloud's phone being down a drain and he thought Cloud was busy talking to someone and that's why his phone was going straight onto voicemail.
"C'mon Cloud answer your fucking phone." Tosh said out loud while trying to call Cloud for the fifth or sixth time since parking his car.
In the Audi Calum was driving while Brian sat in the front passenger seat admiring the knife he had taken from Cloud.
"I've got to admit Cloud's mate Sandy has excellent taste in knives." said Brian calmly as inspected the knife in his hand.
"Do you thinks so?" asked Calum.
"Oh aye. For sure." said Brian.
"It's just a shame I'll have to get rid of it after I use it on Cloud." Brian continued.
Brian had intended to strangle or suffocate Cloud when it came time to kill him but now that he had a good knife in his hands he decided he would just slit his throat instead.
"Where do we go now?" asked Calum.
"Your place. I want to dismantle and remove the Stingray before we take this car away to get burnt out" said Brian.
"OK" replied Calum.
20 minutes later Calum was parking the Audi in his driveway behind his Porsche.
"We need to swap seats." said Brian.
Calum and Brian both got out the car and walked around the front of the vehicle and got in the opposite front doors from what they had just got out. Brian got in the driver side

and Calum got in the front passenger side.
Brian immediately started dismantling the cradle attached to the dashboard that held the Stingray display interface tablet in place.
"Get the bag from the back seat." Brian said to Calum.
Calum reached back between the front seats and picked up the sports bag from the back seat and put it in his lap.
"Now get the 2 walkie-talkies from the bag and put them at your feet." said Brian.
Calum rummaged around in the bag with his right hand and pulled out Brian's Glock in a holster. He looked at the gun for a few seconds then put it back in. A few seconds later Calum took out a walkie-talkie radio then a few seconds later he took out the other and placed them both at his feet in the flooring area of the passenger side of the Audi.
"Now unplug the Ethernet cable and the power cable from the Stingray and put the Stingray in the bag." Brian continued as he removed the tablet interface from the cradle.
Calum did as Brian asked and quickly unplugged the Ethernet cable, then the power cable from the Stingray then put the Stingray unit in the sports bag on his lap.
Brian unplugged the Ethernet cable from the tablet, unplugged the power cable from the cigarette lighter, wrapped both cables around a few times then handed them both to Calum.
"Put these in the bag as well." said Brian as he handed the rolled up cables to Calum.
Calum carefully put the cables into the sports bag next to the Stingray unit.
"And this." said Brian as he handed the tablet interface to Calum.
Calum placed the interface tablet into the bag as well.

Brian removed the tablet cradle from the dashboard and placed it in the back seat of the Audi. The cradle was not important enough to go in the sports bag so it would just get burned up when they torch the Audi later.

"Now I'd like you to put the bag in your house for safekeeping. Take a walkie-talkie with you." said Brian.

Calum reached down in the flooring area of the car and picked up a walkie-talkie.

"Switch it on with the volume knob on the top. Press and hold the button on the side to talk." said Brian.

Calum turned the walkie-talkie on via the volume knob on the top of the device then got out the car carrying the sports bag in one hand and the walkie-talkie in the other and made his way along the driveway towards the front door of his house.

Calum placed the sports bag on the top step of the steps that lead to his front door, reached into his front pocket, took out his keys then opened the door with the keys, picked up the sports bag again and walked into his house.

The alarm in Calum's house started beeping loudly so Calum quickly walked over to the alarm panel on the left hand side wall further along the corridor and typed in the six-digit security code to disarm the alarm.

Calum slowly walked along the corridor into his kitchen, switched on the kitchen light and placed the sports bag onto the island in the kitchen.

As soon as Calum placed the bag on the island the walkie-talkie he was carrying came to life.

"Testing. Testing. One two. Do you hear me OK Calum?" asked Brian's voice over the walkie-talkie.

Calum held the walkie-talkie up to his mouth and pressed the button on the side of it.

"I hear you fine Brian." said Calum.

"Good. Are you good to go?" said Brian over the walkie-talkie.
"Good to go." replied Calum as he walked back towards the front door stopping for a few seconds to reset the burglar alarm via the control panel on the wall.
When Calum got outside he was greeted by Brian standing between Calum's Porsche and the stolen Audi.
"You need to take the battery out of your phone." said Brian as he held up right hand with holding his own disassembled phone for Calum to see.
"Your phone leaves a track of everywhere you go even when its switched off." explained Brian as Calum took his phone out of his front jeans pocket and took it apart.
"From now on we communicate using these." said Brian as he held up his walkie-talkie to face height.
"OK." said Calum in agreement.
"And keep your phone in bits until we get back to Glasgow." said Brian.
Back to Glasgow? Calum wondered where were they going?
Calum decided to ask.
"Where are we going?" asked Calum.
"Bathgate." replied Brian.
"Bathgate?" asked Calum.
"Aye. Bathgate West Lothian." replied Brian.
Calum already knew where Bathgate was. It was near West Calder, the place he took Sarah to meet Donny.
"What's in Bathgate?" asked Calum.
"There's a hilly area on the North East edge of the town that I know and it's ideal for burying a body." said Brian.
"OK." said Calum.
"I'll drive in front in the Audi and you follow me in your Porsche. We'll communicate while we drive using the

walkie-talkies." said Brian.

"Got it." said Calum.

"We'll stick to the speeding limits for the roads we use. We don't want to get pulled over for speeding by any traffic cops," explained Brian.

"It'll take us about 40 minutes along the motorway to get to the Bathgate turn-off and maybe another 20 to get to the Bathgate hills. Cloud should be out cold for at least another 2 or 3 hours so he'll never know what happened to him." Brian said coldly.

"OK." said Calum.

"Let's do this." said Brian as he opened the driver's door on the Audi and got in.

Calum quickly walked over to his Porsche and got into the driver's seat and started his car up.

Brian reversed the Audi out of Calum's driveway and off to the right then forward and away followed closely by Calum in the Porsche.

Thirty minutes later Brian and Calum had been motorway driving for a while on the M8 motorway that leads from Glasgow in the West to Edinburgh in the East with Calum following Brian about 50 feet behind the Audi in his Porsche.

Brian decided to break radio silence. He picked up his radio from the front passenger seat in the Audi and spoke into it.

"How are you doing back there Calum?" Brian asked.

Calum quickly replied.

"I'm good mate. How are you? How's the cargo?" Calum asked.

"I'm good and the cargo is still out cold." said Brian.

There was a pause for a few seconds before Brian spoke again.

"Listen. There's a slight change of plans." Brian started.

"We aren't going as far as Bathgate. We're getting off at the Whitburn turn-off just before Bathgate then we're taking the A801 that runs along the outskirts of Bathgate then we'll access the hills to the North of the town" Brian explained.

Although Brian never explained why he was changing the plans slightly Calum understood why he was doing this. Brian was concerned about getting picked up on CCTV or dash cam footage if he was to take the Bathgate turn-off on the motorway and to drive through the town centre towards the hills to the North.

Calum could see Brian's logic. Better to avoid the town altogether and drive along the outskirts as much as possible.

"Here we go Calum. The next turn-off is ours." said Brian over the radio.

"OK." Calum replied.

Less than a minute later Calum noticed Brian had switched on the left indicator lights on the Audi. He was getting ready to exit the motorway. Calum immediately turned on the left indicator lights on the Porsche and prepared to exit the motorway.

A few seconds later Brian in the Audi and Calum in the Porsche both exited the motorway by the turn-off slip road and stopped at the roundabout that runs underneath the motorway.

Brian switched on the left indicator to tell Calum to follow him along the first exit on the roundabout onto the A801. Calum put on the indicator in the Porsche and followed Brian along the road he had selected.

Calum knew very little of the area they were entering. Apart from visiting Donny recently at the paintballing arena in West Calder, Calum had almost no knowledge of the West Lothian area of Scotland.

He knew a few of the town names because he had seen them mentioned on motorway signs. Livingston, Bathgate, Broxburn, Whitburn and a few others but he knew nothing about these places.

Just a few hundred metres North of the motorway turn-off they approached another roundabout.

"Straight ahead at this roundabout." said Brian over the radio.

"OK." Calum replied.

Both Brian and Calum drove around the roundabout and straight on further down the A801 along a secluded stretch of road that separated the two former mining towns of Bathgate on the right and Armadale on the left.

About a mile and a bit later Brian spoke over the radio again as they approached another roundabout, that lead to Armadale town centre on the left and Bathgate town centre on the right.

"Straight ahead again after this roundabout Calum." said Brian over the radio.

"Got it." replied Calum.

Both Brian and Calum steered their cars around the roundabout and straight onward after the roundabout. Brian spoke over the radio again.

"Calum in a minute or two's time we're going to be leaving this stretch of road. We're going to be taking a right onto the outskirts of Bathgate." Brian said calmly.

"OK." replied Calum.

After the roundabout between Armadale and Bathgate the road split into a dual carriageway then back to a single carriageway then back to a dual carriageway.

A few hundred metres into the second stretch of dual carriageway Brian was approaching the crossing point in the road and Calum saw the right indicators on the Audi start blinking and the red brake lights light up as the car slowed down.

Calum did likewise in the Porsche and slowed down with his indicators blinking and followed behind Brian in the Audi.

It was now after half past 10 at night and the roads were pretty quiet so Brian and Calum could cross the dual carriageway immediately and onto the long winding road that lead from the dual carriageway into the North West corner of Bathgate towards the Bathgate hills.

"When we get into town I won't be able to direct you over the radio. Stay close and just do what I do when I do it." said Brian over the radio.

"No problem." replied Calum.

Calum wondered for a few seconds how Brian knew exactly where to go.

How did he know about the back roads into a relatively small West Lothian mining town?

How did he know about the suitability of the Bathgate hills for disposing of a body?

After a few seconds passed Calum just decided that Brian was a military professional and had probably scouted out the surrounding area before choosing it for the operation. Calum thought of the 6 P's saying that was drummed into all military personnel from day 1 of joining the military.

'Proper Preparation Prevents Piss Poor Performance'.

By now Brian and Calum had passed through the open fields close to the dual carriageway and had reached the inhabited area in North West Bathgate.

It almost entirely consisted of semi-detached council houses with gardens to the front and to the rear and it looked like most people took care of their gardens. All in all it looked like an OK wee place.

Calum concentrated on the black Audi Q5 Brian was driving in front of him ready to go wherever it did.

The road Brian and Calum were driving on curved off to the right slightly until it reached a mini roundabout.

Brian took the second exit from the roundabout going straight forward and switching on his left indicator lights as he moved forward.

Calum did exactly the same.

150 metres or so along the road Brian indicated to turn left, then turned left followed immediately by Calum.

The road they were on went on for another 400 or 500 metres before coming to another mini roundabout.

Again Brian took the second exit from the roundabout, the choice to go straight on and indicated left when leaving the roundabout.

Calum did exactly the same.

The road they were now on was getting more rural again with trees and fields on either side of the road for 600 or 700 metres until it came to a larger roundabout at the top of the slightly inclining road offering a turn to the Bathgate hills and the ancient town of Torphichen on the left or a direct road to the centre of town on the right.

This time Brian indicated left in advance of the roundabout to let Calum know they were heading left.

Both Brian and Calum turned left towards Torphichen and the Bathgate hills and found themselves on another rural road with houses sporadically placed on the right and open fields and a golf course on the left.

After just a couple of minutes Brian indicated right and began to slow down. He had reached the Bathgate hills access road they were going to use. There were many access roads to where they were going but this was the one

Brian had decided to use.

Brian and Calum both started to drive up the fairly steep curvy winding road that lead through the heart of the Bathgate hills, a semi-open fielded and semi forested area of hills.

The surrounding area was a favourite haunt of stolen car joyriders, mountain bikers, weed smokers, dog walkers and criminal gangs looking for a discreet place to hand out a punishment beating or shooting as well as a good place to bury a body.

Calum noticed Brian had slowed down his driving speed quite a bit, probably partly because the road they were driving on was not well suited to high speed driving, and partly because Brian was looking for the right spot for them to do the deed.

Calum knew what Brian was looking for. He was looking for somewhere with access for their cars but wooded over enough for make it impossible for anyone to witness what was happening.

After a few minutes Brian slowed down the Audi and stopped, put on the hazard lights then got out. He had found the spot he was looking for. Calum stopped the car behind Brian and also got out.

Brian was now at the rear of the Audi and opened up the boot then reached over Cloud's unconscious body and picked up the heavy duty bolt cutters Calum had saw him put in the boot earlier that day.

Calum noticed next to where they were parked, there was an access point to a red ash track that ran alongside a heavily wooded area on the right of the track.

The access point to the track gated off with a heavy wooden double gate held closed by an equally heavy padlock but that wasn't going to be a problem.

Brian stepped over to the gate and cut the padlock with a single motion with the bolt cutters then pushed open the gate.

Brian quickly shook off the remaining part of the padlock and tossed it aside into the long grass that ran along the side of the road.

"I'll drive in first. You follow me. Close the gate behind you when you drive in." said Brian as he walked back to the Audi.

"OK." said Calum as he nodded in agreement.

Brian started up the Audi, reversed back and to the right a little then turned left onto the red ash track. Calum followed closely in the Porsche.

Calum stopped his car 20 metres or so along the track, quickly got out, walked back to close the gate then got back into his car and followed Brian.

The track they were driving on was made up of red shale and ash and was designed to be used by tractors pulling large trailer loads of timber so it was plenty wide enough for the Audi and the Porsche.

100 metres or so along the track Brian stopped the Audi and got out. Calum immediately stopped his car and got out.

"This'll do nicely" said Brian clipping his radio onto his belt and the sheathed hunting knife down the back of his jeans.

Calum quickly looked at the surrounding area. On the left of the road was wide open and had a downhill gradient and on the right was a densely forested area full of pine trees.

Brian opened up the boot of the Audi, took out the spade he put in there earlier and leaned it against the side of the car. He then leaned forward into the boot area, picked up the still unconscious Cloud placing him across his shoulders then he picked up the spade and started walking towards the wooded area on the right.

"I shouldn't be more than half an hour. If you need me get me on the radio." said Brian as he walked past Calum carrying Cloud and the spade.

"OK" said Calum as he stood between the 2 cars.

In less than a minute Brian found himself in a fairly dark and dense forest. Although it was still quite light outside the wooded area, it was pretty dark in it because of the densely packed trees blocking out the light.

Everything was brown. The tree trunks and their roots were brown and the ground was carpeted in dead brown pine needles that crunched under Brian's feet as he walked through the forested area.

It was dark but not too dark for Brian as he could see exactly what he was doing and that's all that mattered.

After a minute or two of walking carefully through the wooded area Brian had picked out a spot to bury Cloud's body.

The spot he picked out was a small clearing in the forest floor just a few metres long and a few metres wide where ferns had taken advantage of the sunlight leaking through the canopy from an empty space caused by a tree being blown over in high winds and had the ferns had flourished into a patch of green in an otherwise brown forest floor. Brian would dig out a hole in the centre of the fern patch 6 feet long by 3 feet wide and 3 feet deep. He would also take care not to damage the roots of the ferns he was digging out as he planned to replant them exactly where he found them so over time they could feed and flourish on Cloud's decomposing body.

Brian kneeled down and rolled Cloud off his shoulders and onto the forest floor. Cloud landed on his back and let out a

loud groan as he hit the ground.
Brian paused for a few seconds watching over Cloud. Brian knew it was unlikely Cloud was waking up as just little over an hour ago Brian had injected Cloud full of enough sedatives to put a horse to sleep for a few hours. It was unlikely but not impossible.
What if Cloud had built up a high tolerance for sedatives because of regular use of downers?
After a few seconds of no more movement from Cloud Brian started the task at hand. Digging a grave for Cloud. Brian started digging at the centre of the fern patch taking care to pick up each individual divot at first and placing it aside trying not to damage the roots too much as he wanted them to continue growing as soon as possible feeding on Cloud's body.
About 20 minutes later Brian finished digging the grave for Cloud and stood over it for a few seconds. The grave was exactly what was required for the job. It was a 6 feet long, 3 feet wide, 3 feet deep and surrounded by ferns.
Brian stuck the spade into the ground and approached Cloud's unconscious body lying nearby.
Brian picked up Cloud's unconscious body by the crutch and upper chest area on his clothing and carried him a few metres then placed him on his back next to the grave.
Brian paused for a few seconds over Cloud then placed his right foot on Cloud's right ribs and pushed him over into the grave landing face down in the hole.
Brian stepped down into the grave and stood on Cloud's back. He took the hunting knife out of its sheath in the back of his jeans and placed his left knee on the back of Cloud's neck. He then reached down over Cloud's forehead and put his left gloved hand into Cloud's eye sockets and pulled his head back as far as it would go. Brian then took the knife in

his right hand and stabbed it deep into the left hand side of Cloud's throat then forcefully dragged it to the other side of his throat almost decapitating Cloud in the process.

Brian stepped out of the grave to watch Cloud die.

The blood was pouring from Cloud's throat wound, his body was convulsing as if he was taking some kind of fit and he was making a horrible gargling sound as he choked on his own blood.

After 30 seconds or so the gargling and convulsions had stopped. Cloud was dead.

Brian grabbed the spade and began filling in the grave with loose soil at first and then he placed the ferns on top of the gravesite and stamped them down into place with his right foot to help them flourish.

2 minutes later Brian emerged from the forested area carrying the spade over his right shoulder.

"Job done?" asked Calum as Brian approached the cars where Calum was standing.

"Job done." stated Brian as he opened the right rear passenger door of the Audi and placed first the spade and then the sheathed hunting knife in the backseat.

"Now what?" asked Calum.

"Now we burn the Audi then head home" said Brian.

"OK" replied Calum and got into his Porsche.

Brian did likewise and got into the Audi.

Calum carefully reversed the Porsche the 80 or so metres along the red ash track to the point he had to stop to open the heavy wooden gate and stopped his car about 20 metres away from the gate and got out and left the car engine running.

Calum quickly walked over to the gate and opened it fully for him and Brian to get out and equally quickly made it made it back to his Porsche and continued reversing out the ash track and back onto the tarmac main road.

Calum reversed off to his left to allow Brian to get the larger Audi out and onto the road.

As soon as Brian had backed the Audi out of the ash track and onto the tarmac main road he parked the car up, got out the car, closed the gate and got back into his car.

Brian picked up the radio from the front seat and held it up to his mouth to speak to Calum.

"We need to find a spot to torch this car. Follow me. I'll pick out a wee layby somewhere." he said.

"Cool." replied Calum over the radio.

Brian pulled the Audi away and started to slowly make his way along the road further into the hills towards the tourist town of Linlithgow.

Brian didn't want to go as far as Linlithgow. Too many CCTV cameras too many dash cams on other cars. He wanted to dispose of the car up in the hills then go back to Glasgow exactly the way came.

Through the outskirts of Bathgate then onto the dual carriageway then onto the motorway then home to Glasgow.

Brian quickly scanned both sides of the road in front of him for a layby to park and torch the Audi. He didn't have to search for long as these roads were designed to include a layby every few hundred metres to allow larger vehicles to pass on a fairly narrow road.

After a few minutes Brian found what he was looking for. A small layby ideal for burning a vehicle.

"Here we go. This'll do nicely." said Brian over the radio as he pulled into the small layby on the road.

Calum pulled his car in behind him, got out and approached the driver door of the Audi to speak to Brian.

"So how do you want to do this?" asked Calum.

"You drive on and turn your car around first chance you get and come back here. When you get back I'll torch this car and we'll leave the same way we came." said Brian.
"OK cool." replied Calum before walking back to his car, getting in and driving off.
Calum didn't have to drive far to find somewhere to turn his car around. About 200 metres along the road there was a small junction that lead further into the forested area of the hills they were in. Perfect for quickly turning a car around.
Calum slowed his car down as he passed the junction, stopped his car then quickly reversed into the junction then forwards again back towards Brian and the Audi.
Back at the Audi, Brian was waiting for Calum and Calum flashed his lights at Brian as he approached to let him know it was him. Calum parked his Porsche in behind the Audi facing the opposite way back towards Bathgate.
Brian immediately lowered both the front and both the rear car windows via the window control switch in the driver's door and got out the car. He then went to the rear of the car and opened up the boot and took out the green petrol can he had put in there earlier.
Brian then unscrewed the top from the petrol can and quickly doused the inside of the boot with petrol. Then he moved on to the rear right hand door leaving the boot open and opened the rear right car door and quickly doused the back seat on the right with petrol. Next he opened the driver door and doused the driver seat thoroughly with petrol. Then he moved onto the front passenger door then the left rear door opening each door in turn and dousing the inside of the car with petrol.
All in all the process of dousing the entire inside of the car took less than 1 minute to do.

After using up the last of the petrol on the rear left side of the car Brian placed the petrol can on the back seat of the car then walked over to the rear right of the car, reached into his front jeans pocket and took out a packet of matches and paused for a few seconds.

After a few seconds Brian lit one of the matched and placed the lit match back into the box causing all the matches to flare up and he gently threw the flaming box into the back seat of the car through the opened right rear window.

Almost immediately the car was engulfed in flames as the petrol ignited.

Brian calmly walked over to Calum's waiting car and got in the passenger side then Calum drove off back the way they came. Calum watched the burning car in his rear view mirror as long as he could.

Sooner or later someone would report the burning car to the police or the fire brigade and the car would be extinguished then removed and written off by the cops as just another joyrider disposing of a stolen car.

All the way home Brian said very little. In fact, the only time he spoke to Calum was when they were parked up in Calum's driveway.

Calum parked his car, got out and started walking towards Calum's house. Brian did likewise as he wanted to get his sports bag with the Stingray and his kit in it.

"When do you think your man McGurk will make a move on Sned?" he asked referring to Calum's contact in the prison beside the last remaining name on his hit list.

Calum put his key in the keyhole and opened the door before answering.

"Well I posted him a letter this morning so he should get it tomorrow morning and if I know McGurk he'll make a move first chance he gets. Probably within 24 hours of reading my letter" replied Calum.

Calum's house alarm started making beeping sounds and Calum quickly made his way to the control panel on the left hand side wall and typed in his security code to disarm the alarm.

"OK. Keep your ear to the ground and let me know as soon as you hear anything." said Brian as he entered Calum's house.

"Will do mate." said Calum.

Calum quickly made his way along the corridor towards his kitchen and walked back carrying Brian's sports bag with his kit in it.

Calum handed the bag to Brian.

Brian started to walk away but stopped for a second.

"And one more thing," Brian started.

"Thanks for your help." he continued and reached out to shake Calum's hand.

"It was my pleasure." said Calum as he shook Brian's hand.

Brian walked out of Calum's house and walked away down the driveway towards the road outside.

Calum opened up his fridge, took out a bottle of mineral water then reached into his front jeans pocket to gather the parts of his disassembled phone.

He thought it would be a good idea to let Sarah know he was home OK as he knew she was worried about him.

Calum quickly assembled his phone on the island in his kitchen.

First the battery, then the phone case and then the rubber protective case.

Calum pressed the power on button on the side of the phone and the small apple logo lit up on the screen.

After 20 or 30 or so seconds the phone booted up and immediately started making pinging sounds alerting him to the receipt of SMS text messages.

There were 4 messages in total all from Sarah.

Calum started to read the messages.

The first message read – "phone or txt me when u get a chance".

The second message read – "phone or txt me".

The third message read – "phone or txt me asap".

The fourth and final message read – "please phone or txt me when u get a chance I need to know ur OK".

Calum looked at his watch.

It was nearly 12.30am.

Too late to call Sarah.

He would just send her a text message.

Calum quickly typed out a text message to Sarah.

The message he typed read –

"That's me home now I'm fine. Mission accomplished".

Calum sent the text message and started to get out his car.

Within 20 seconds of sending Sarah a text message Calum's phone started ringing. Calum looked at his phone.

It was Sarah calling.

"Hello?" said Calum as he held the phone to his ear.

"Thank God you're OK." said Sarah standing in the middle of her living room in her pyjamas.

"I'm fine Sarah. I'm fine." said Calum trying to reassure Sarah that everything was good.

"Did everything go to plan?" asked Sarah remembering not to say much over the telephone.

"Aye everything went to plan. Everything is fine." said Calum.

"When will I see you?" asked Sarah.

"I'll pick you up tomorrow morning at half past nine at the usual place." said Calum.

"Good. That's good. I'll see you then." said Sarah feeling

reassured after speaking to Calum.
"I'll see you then," replied Calum as he ended the call.
"And Sarah." Calum continued.
"What?" asked Sarah.
"Bring your laptop." Calum added.
"OK." said Sarah.

chapter twelve

Wednesday. 9.30am. South Glasgow

It was another rainy morning in South Glasgow and Calum was parked at the bus stop across the road from Sarah's flat. The windscreen wipers intermittently wiped the rain away from the front window and Calum's fingers tapped on the steering wheel in time with the pop song playing on the radio.

Within a minute of parking up Calum saw Sarah approaching the car from the other side of the road underneath a small black umbrella and carrying her laptop bag in her other hand.

Sarah quickly crossed the road and got into the passenger door of Calum's car.

"I'm so glad to see that you're OK," said Sarah as she placed her laptop bag and her umbrella at her feet and sat in the passenger seat of Calum's car.

"I was so worried about you. I thought that Brian was going to kill you and when you wouldn't answer your phone or reply to my text messages that just made me worry more." said Sarah getting emotional.

"I'm fine Sarah. There's no need to worry about me." said Calum as he drove his car out of the bus stop area and back towards his home.

A minute or so passed before Sarah spoke up.

"So what happened with Cloud?" she asked.

Calum paused before answering.

"It's probably better that you don't know." said Calum

coldly.

"OK cool. You're right. I don't know anything and don't want to know anything." Sarah replied.

Another minute or so passed before Sarah spoke up again. "So where are we going?" she asked.

"My place. We're going to my place. We've got a story to write. A story about a tit for tat power struggle within the CYT that ended in 4 murders." said Calum.

"And Cloud was guilty of the fourth and final murder?" asked Sarah.

"And he's ran away before the cops can talk to him?" Sarah continued.

"That's right." said Calum.

"And Cloud is never going to turn up and try to clear his name?" said Sarah stating the obvious.

"No. He's not." said Calum.

"OK. No problem," said Sarah.

"No problem at al.l" she continued.

25 minutes later Calum and Sarah were entering Calum's house with Calum quickly walking along the hall to disarm the burglar alarm via the control panel on the left hand side wall. Sarah followed behind him carrying her laptop bag. Calum and Sarah entered Calum's kitchen area and Sarah immediately placed her laptop bag down on the kitchen island while Calum opened up his fridge.

"Do you want anything to drink" he asked.

"Mineral water? Fruit juice? Irn bru?" he continued.

"I'll have a mineral water please." said Sarah.

Calum took 2 bottles of mineral water out his fridge and walked over to the island where Sarah was standing and taking her laptop out of the bag and handed her a bottle of water.

"Thanks." said Sarah as she unscrewed the lid from the

bottle.
Calum reached into a storage area under the island and took out 2 barstool type seats and offered one to Sarah.
"Thanks." said Sarah as she sat on one of the seats.

Sarah switched her laptop on and waited a few seconds for it to boot up.
Calum looked at his watch.
"Have you got an appointment?" asked Sarah.
"What?" asked Calum.
"Your watch. That's about the fifth time you've looked at it since you picked me up. Do you need to be somewhere?" she asked.
"No. No I don't need to be somewhere. I'm just waiting for the last piece of a puzzle to fall into place" said Calum.
The last piece of a puzzle Calum was talking about was that prisoners in HMP Barlinnie usually receive their mail between 10 and 11 am so Tam McGurk should be receiving the letter Calum wrote him anytime now.

Wednesday. 10.30am. North East Glasgow

It was mail time at HMP Barlinnie and Officer Higgins was on mail duty handing out mail to the inmates in D hall. Officer Higgins was dressed in the usual prison officer attire of black shoes and trousers, white half-sleeved shirt and clip on tie. He whistled as he made his way along the walkway on the second floor with cells on his left and metal fencing along the right.

All the mail had been scanned for weapons and sniffed for drugs before being handed out to the inmates.

Officer Higgins stopped outside the cell Tam McGurk shared with another inmate, Bobby O'Brian, and poked his head into the cell to see McGurk lying on the bottom of 2 bunk beds in the cell. Bobby O'Brian was not in the cell at that time.

McGurk was 6 foot 4 and 25 stone and had his dark brown hair shaved short and he sported a goatee beard.

"You've got mail McGurk" said Officer Higgins as he reached out to McGurk with an envelope in his hand.

McGurk quickly got off the bed and approached Officer Higgins and reached out to receive the envelope.

"Thanks boss" said McGurk as he walked back to the bed carrying the envelope.

McGurk sat back down on his bed, opened the envelope and began to read the enclosed letter.

Wednesday. 1.30pm. West Glasgow.

Calum and Sarah were sitting down at opposite sides of a large circular dining table in Calum's Italian themed restaurant Francesco's in Glasgow's trendy West End.

The restaurant consisted of 14 large circular tables each approximately 5 feet in diameter and big enough to comfortably sit 6 people at each table.

Each table was covered in a white silk table cloth and all around the restaurant there were life-sized replica marble statues of various Roman and Greek deities.

Large but tasteful chandeliers hung from the ceiling and there was a bar area at the rear of the restaurant with waist high bar stools along the side of it.

The entire restaurant was busy with all of the dining tables filled to capacity and all of the bar stools were in use with people waiting for a table to become available.

Several suited waiters skilfully walked and weaved between the tables bringing food and drinks and bills to the customers.

Both Calum and Sarah were looking through a menu each. Nino, the waiter that served them the last time they ate there, stood leaning against the bar patiently waiting for a signal from Calum to come and take their orders.

"Thanks for taking me out for lunch. I appreciate it." said Sarah from behind her menu.

"It's my pleasure." said Calum.

"It's just what I was needing. A wee break from writing up our piece." started Sarah.

Sarah lowered her menu onto the table in front of her and leaned into the table to speak quietly to Calum.

"Who knew concocting a work of complete fiction would be so stressful?" Sarah continued.

"Believable bullshit Sarah. That's all we need to produce. A piece of believable bullshit." said Calum.
"Right," said Sarah as she leaned back into her seat.
"Believable bullshit. That's all we need." Sarah continued.
Calum placed his menu down on the table in front of him.
"I'm ready to order. What about you?" he asked.
"I'm good. I'll just have what I had the last time I was here." stated Sarah.
"OK then." said Calum as he gave Nino the thumbs up signal the waiter was waiting for.
Calum and Sarah would enjoy a nice meal and then head back to Calum's place to finish off their story to be emailed to Bobby McCiver as soon as it was ready as he requested at their last meeting.

Wednesday. 4.30pm. North East Glasgow

It was almost dinner time in D hall at Barlinnie prison and Rab Cook, known as Cooky, made his way along the second floor pathway towards the cell he shared with Sned. At 35 he was more than 10 years older than Sned but he knew Sned well as they were both junkies from the same area of Glasgow, they both moved in the same circles and had both been in and out of prison and young offender institutions their entire lives.

He was slimly built with short blonde hair, his forearms were covered in prison tattoos and he walked with an unjustifiable swagger that only came after a lifetime of prison experience.

He nodded his head at other inmates he passed as he walked along the pathway and said "alright mate" to others until he reached his cell.

The cell door was closed so Cooky had to shove it open. Cooky opened the door and walked into the cell. Sned was lying on his back in the bottom bunk with a pillow over his face.

Cooky kicked the bunk bed gently to wake Sned.

"Wakey wakey Sned it's almost dinner time" said Cooky.

Sned didn't react.

Cooky sat on the bed next to Sned and gently shook him by the shoulder.

"C'mon mate. Time for a feed"

Again Sned didn't react.

Cooky gently picked up the pillow that was covering Sned's face to wake Sned up.

The underside of the pillow, the side that was on Sned's face, was completely soaked in blood, Sned's face was completely smashed in and Sned wasn't breathing.

Sned was dead. He had been beaten unrecognisable and then smothered to death.

Cooky dropped the pillow onto the floor and held his hands over his face in shock.

chapter thirteen

Thursday. 10.30am. Daily Post HQ. Glasgow.

Calum and Sarah were sitting in seats in the hallway outside Bobby McCiver's office. Sarah was dressed in a smart trouser suit with 3 inch heels and Calum was dressed in a suit and white shirt with no tie.
It was a busy newspaper environment. All around them people rushed around talking into mobile phones while others carried sheets of paper or folders.
Sarah had emailed their story to Bobby McCiver at about 9.30 last night and received a reply about an hour later telling them both to report to his office at 10.30 the following morning.
Calum could see Sarah was nervous as her foot was tapping on the floor and she was also holding on tightly with both hands to her small handbag in her lap.
Calum reached over and placed his hand onto both of hers.
"Relax. We've done nothing wrong. Well you've done nothing wrong. He doesn't suspect anything. We're in the clear. Just let me do the talking when we get in there." he said gently to Sarah trying to reassure her.
"OK," said Sarah.
"I can do that." she continued.
Just then Bobby's office door opened and Bobby poked his head around the corner to face Calum and Sarah.
"C'mon in guys" he said to them both.
Calum and Sarah got up and walked into Bobby's office. Bobby sat down on his large swivel chair and gestured for

Calum and Sarah to sit on two smaller swivel chairs on the near side of the desk.

"Please sit down guys." he said to Calum and Sarah.

Calum and Sarah sat down into the chairs in front of Bobby's desk.

"Well guys I read your piece on these CYT murders last night. Actually I read it 3 or 4 times," Bobby started.

Bobby leaned back into his chair.

"And I thought it was one of the best pieces of investigative journalism I've ever read." Bobby continued.

"Thanks." said Calum.

"Thank you." said Sarah.

"It opened my eyes to a world I never knew existed. The world of murderous rivalries inside a street gang." said Bobby.

"I'm glad. I mean we're glad you liked it." said Calum.

"We've got ahead of every other newspaper in the country and even the police with this. I emailed a copy of your work over to a friend in Police Scotland and they didn't have a clue about any of this stuff either." said Bobby.

"OK." said Calum.

"And this guy Macleod that you've named as the prime suspect in the last murder, the one in the Craigy Inn, has done a runner?" asked Bobby.

"Aye. We believe so. I think we spooked him when we confronted him on his doorstep. I think he's took a few days to gather some money together before disappearing somewhere." said Calum.

"Any ideas where?" asked Bobby.

"Your guess is as good as mine," replied Calum.

"Maybe Liverpool maybe London. Maybe Spain maybe Australia." Calum continued.

"And there won't be any more murders?" asked Bobby.

"No there won't." answered Calum.
"I just can't make up my mind what to do with this story. Do I just publish it all in one or do I serialise it with an instalment every Sunday over 3 or 4 weeks?" said Bobby.
"That's entirely up to you mate." said Calum.
"I do know one thing though. I want the two of you working together full time. You make a hell of a team." said Bobby.
"OK." said Calum.
"Fine with me." said Sarah.
"OK now the both of you should take the rest of the day off. You've earned it. I'll get in touch when I want you to investigate something." said Bobby.
"Cool." said Calum.
"Thanks." said Sarah.
Calum and Sarah both stood up and walked out of Bobby's office.
A couple of minutes later the elevator door to the underground carpark at the Daily Post headquarters opened up and Sarah and Calum stepped out.
All around them were the cars of the newspaper's employees ranging from very small Minis through to the very large Range Rovers and everything in-between.
Calum and Sarah started walking to where Calum had parked his car.
Sarah quickly looked around to make sure no-one was in earshot.
"Are you sure we're in the clear Calum?" she asked.
"What do you mean?" asked Calum.
"Are you sure that no-one from the CYT will go to the cops and tell them everything we wrote about them was total BS?" asked Sarah.
"Yes I'm sure," said Calum.

"None of the CYT would ever go to the cops about anything and even if they did the cops wouldn't believe a word that came out of their mouths." Calum continued. Calum and Sarah had reached Calum's car. Calum disarmed the car alarm with his key fob and both Calum and Sarah got into the car.

As soon as he sat down Calum's phone started ringing so Calum took the phone out of his front trouser pocket and looked at the display. It was Brian calling.

"It's Brian" said Calum.

"Hello?" said Calum into the phone.

"Are you able to talk freely?" Brian asked.

"Aye. I'm in my car in the carpark at work. I'm with my workmate Sarah and she's cool. I can talk in front of her." said Calum.

"Does Sarah have a smart phone?" asked Brian.

"Aye" replied Calum.

"Tell her to go to the BBC news website." said Brian.

"Go to the BBC news website on your phone." Calum said to Sarah.

Sarah quickly got her phone out of her handbag and accessed the BBC news website.

"OK got it." said Sarah.

"OK got it." Calum said to Brian.

"Now tell her to click on the Scotland option in the top left hand corner of the screen." said Brian.

"Click on the Scotland option in the top left hand corner of the screen." Calum repeated to Sarah.

"OK done it." said Sarah.

"OK done it." Calum repeated to Brian.

"Now tell her to click on the second story from the left. The one that says murder in Barlinnie and read it out loud" said Brian.

"Click on the second story from the left. The one that says murder in Barlinnie and read it out loud." Calum repeated to Sarah.

Sarah began to read out the article to Calum.

"Police Scotland has launched a murder inquiry after an inmate was found dead in his cell at H.M.P. Barlinnie yesterday afternoon. The inmate has been named as Mark Sneddon aged 23 from the Craiglen area of Glasgow and he had suffered what the police are calling an horrific and brutal attack." Sarah read out for Calum.

"Looks like your man McGurk is everything you said he was." said Brian.

"Aye. He is." replied Calum.

"I want you to know I appreciate the help you gave me. I'd have struggled without you." said Brian.

"It was no problem at all." said Calum.

"This is the last time you will hear from me so you might as well delete this number from your phone." said Brian.

"OK will do." said Calum.

"I'm looking forward to reading your article in the post about what's been going on." said Brian.

"It'll be in Sunday's edition. It might be serialised over several weeks." said Calum.

"Whatever format it comes in I'll read it. I have an avid interest in this breaking story." said Brian.

The End

Printed in Dunstable, United Kingdom

70218316R00147